"He doesn'[...]

"Well, he . . . um . . . [...]," Sabrina blurted out to [...]

"Purple is my favorite color," Kurt exclaimed.

Roxie knew her hair was dark brown. So Kurt had to be talking about her outfit. Her shirt was red. Her jeans were blue. No purple anywhere. "Is he color-blind?" she whispered to Sabrina.

"Um . . . yeah. Color-blind. That's it . . . yeah." Sabrina agreed.

"Want to share a soda?" Kurt interrupted.

"'Share a soda'?" Roxie whispered. "What is he, cheap or something?"

"He's just being cute," Sabrina whispered back. She turned to Kurt. "Come on, Kurt. You can help me get the sodas."

Sabrina and Kurt walked toward the nearest soda counter. "Kurt, you almost blew it," she warned. "You've got to stop talking."

Kurt nodded. "Let's party!" he said.

Sabrina rolled her eyes. "No partying. You have to keep quiet."

"Purple is my favorite color," Kurt answered.

Now Sabrina was getting annoyed. "If you don't stop talking, I'm going to take out your sound chip," she threatened.

Kurt got the message.

Sabrina, the Teenage Witch™ books

Available from Simon & Schuster

Sabrina The Teenage Witch™

What a Doll!

Nancy Krulik

Based upon the characters in Archie Comics

**And based upon the television series
Sabrina, The Teenage Witch
Created for television by Nell Scovell
Developed for television by Jonathan Schmock**

POCKET
BOOKS

LONDON • NEW YORK • SYDNEY

For Danny, a living doll

**POCKET
BOOKS**

First published in Great Britain 2003 by Pocket Books
An imprint of Simon & Schuster UK Ltd
Africa House, 64–78 Kingsway
London WC2B 6AH

Originally published in the USA in 2003 by Simon Pulse,
an imprint of Simon & Schuster Children's Publishing Division,
New York

POCKET BOOKS and colophon are registered
trademarks of Simon & Schuster
A CIP catalogue record for this book is
available from the British Library

ISBN 0 7434 6257 2

1 3 5 7 9 10 8 6 4 2

Printed and bound in Great Britain by
Bookmarque Ltd, Croydon, Surrey

☆

Chapter 1

☆

"Oooo! This is so frustrating!" Sabrina Spellman shouted as she threw the thick holiday mail-order catalog across the living room.

"Whoa!" Her roommate, Roxie King, ducked just in time to see the catalog sail over her head. That was close. *Too close*. "Watch where you're throwing stuff, will ya?"

Sabrina blushed sheepishly. "Sorry. It's just that I'm so mad at that thing."

"You're mad at a catalog?" Roxie asked sarcastically. "I can sympathize. Just yesterday I had a huge argument with an envelope that said, 'You may have just won a million dollars.' Mail can be such a tease."

Sabrina giggled despite herself. Roxie was right: She *did* sound kind of ridiculous.

1

"So what did the big, bad catalog do to you?" Roxie asked.

"I'm looking for a Halloween costume and there's nothing in there but pumpkins, skeletons, and witches." Sabrina pouted.

"So?" Roxie picked up the catalog and thumbed through the pictures. "I think these witch costumes are kind of cool. All dark and scary—isn't that what Halloween's all about?"

"Witches aren't all—," Sabrina began. Then she stopped herself and sighed. There was no way she could explain to Roxie that witches weren't at all like the costumes in the catalog—not without revealing her secret, anyway. And this secret was a whopper.

Sabrina Spellman was a witch.

Which was how Sabrina knew that witches were pretty much like anyone else. Some were ugly; some were beautiful. Some were nice; and some were evil. Sabrina personally had never seen any witch wearing a ratty black dress and a pointy hat, or riding around on a broomstick. In fact, many of the witches Sabrina knew preferred haute couture and flew across the sky on state-of-the-art vacuum cleaners.

"No, I mean it. You'd make a cute witch," Roxie continued.

"Thanks, anyway," Sabrina moaned.

"I don't understand why this whole Halloween thing is such a big deal to you, anyway," Roxie said.

"Are you kidding?" Sabrina declared. "Halloween is the greatest holiday! My aunts and I have such fun at Halloween. I look forward to it all year long. We put up decorations and sing Halloween songs. Of course, the best part is giving the treats to all our visitors. Halloween really is all about the spirit of giving."

"You make it sound like Christmas," Roxie said.

Sabrina nodded. In the Spellman household, Halloween was as big a deal as Christmas was in other people's houses. It sort of came with being part of a witch family.

"Come on, didn't you love Halloween as a kid?" Sabrina asked Roxie.

Roxie shook her head. "Halloween was no big deal in the King house," she assured Sabrina. "The day after Halloween was more important."

Sabrina looked curiously at Roxie. "The day *after* Halloween?" she repeated.

"Yeah," Roxie said. "See, we didn't have enough money to buy candy or anything. So when kids came by and said 'Trick or Treat,' we had to choose

3

the trick. And believe me, those kids could play some heavy-duty tricks. My family spent the day after Halloween scrubbing rotten eggs off the car, unsticking the pins in our doorbell, and ripping down toilet paper from the trees."

Sabrina frowned. Roxie's childhood stories never ceased to amaze her. "Well, this Halloween is going to be great. I mean, how lucky were we to get invited to the Sigma Kappa Delta Halloween Howler tomorrow night? Have you decided what you're going to wear?"

Roxie shook her head and opened her mouth to speak. But before she could get a word out, Morgan Cavanaugh, the girls' resident adviser, came bursting into the house. She was carrying a small, pink pocketbook and smiling brightly as though she didn't have a care in the world.

Trailing behind her was Harvey Kinkle—at least Sabrina *thought* it was Harvey. It was hard to tell since his face was completely hidden by the huge stack of department store boxes and bags he was carrying.

"Look who I ran into at the mall," Morgan said cheerfully. "Wasn't it lucky that Harvey came along just in time to help me carry my packages?"

Sabrina shook her head. Harvey and Morgan had dated for a while earlier in the school year. They were broken up now, but Morgan still treated Harvey like her boyfriend—which basically meant she treated him like a slave. And for some reason Sabrina would never understand, Harvey let her.

"What's all that?" Roxie asked Morgan.

"They're necessities," Morgan assured her. Ever since Morgan's dad had cut off her credit cards, she'd had to be more careful with her cash.

Roxie opened one of the bags and pulled out a brand-new hair dryer. "This seems like a real necessity," she said sarcastically. "What a tough decision you must have had. Do I spend my money on food and shelter, or great hair?"

The sarcasm was lost on Morgan. "My point exactly," she agreed.

"So you chose the hair," Roxie mused.

"Well, you don't expect me to go to the Sigma Kappa Delta Halloween Howler with a frizzy head, do you?" Morgan insisted. "It's not like I'm one of you two."

Sabrina eyed Morgan suspiciously. "Excuse me?"

Morgan rolled her eyes. "People expect me to look good. There would be a huge uproar if I showed up at the Halloween Howler with bad hair. How awful would that be? It could ruin the whole party."

Sabrina bit her lip to keep from laughing. It was hard to believe that Morgan actually believed what she was saying. But she did. "So what costume are you wearing to the party?" Sabrina asked, changing the subject as quickly as she could.

"I know who I'm going as—," Harvey announced.

"How can you know if I haven't told you yet?" Morgan interrupted incredulously. "I was going to keep it a surprise until tomorrow, but now that you've brought it up . . ." She reached into one of her boxes and pulled out two costumes. One was a magnificent ball gown that looked like something right out of the Italian Renaissance. The other costume was a pair of royal blue tights, with a matching blue-and-gold tunic

"This one's mine," she said, holding up the gown. "And that one's yours."

Harvey stared at the tights. "What kind of costume is that?"

Morgan giggled. "A prince costume," she said. "We're going as Romeo and Juliet. She reached into another bag. "And see, you get to carry a sword. Won't that be fun?"

"I'm not going to the party in tights," Harvey told her. "I'm going to be the Scarecrow from *The Wizard of Oz*."

"No, you're not," Morgan scoffed. "I already rented the costumes for us."

Harvey sighed. "Morgan. There is no 'us.' We broke up, remember?"

Morgan shrugged. "That doesn't mean we can't go to the party together, does it?" she asked with sugary sweetness dripping in her voice. "I mean, we're still friends, right?"

"Sure," Harvey agreed. "We can go together. But I'm not wearing that outfit."

Suddenly, all the candy-coated kindness disappeared from Morgan's tone. It was replaced with seething venom. "Oh, yes you are, Harvey Kinkle!" Morgan shouted. "You'll do what I tell you to."

Sabrina waited for Harvey to tell Morgan to go jump in a lake, but he didn't. He just stood there, staring at those blue tights.

"Why should he listen to you?" Sabrina jumped to Harvey's defense. She and Harvey had been friends since high school. There was no way she was going to let Morgan talk to him that way.

"Because he owes me," Morgan replied simply.

"For what?" Sabrina demanded.

"For dating him, of course."

"What are you talking about?" Sabrina replied. "Harvey's a really nice guy. You were lucky to have gone out with him."

"Harvey is nice," Morgan agreed. "But I'm more popular. When I started dating Harvey, his social status rose about a billion notches. He became a hot campus commodity. You know, popularity by association." Morgan turned to Harvey. "You will be my Romeo," she said sternly. "No arguments. I brought you into the world of popularity, and I can take you out of it."

Harvey didn't say anything. He just picked up the tights and sat down on the couch.

"That's better," Morgan said sweetly. "And don't worry—the blue is going to look so great with your eyes. You're going to make an adorable Romeo, Harvey. I'm so glad we're friends." With that, Morgan swept off into her room, taking her blow dryer with her. "Well, I'm off to diffuse," she announced.

As soon as Morgan left the room, Sabrina and Roxie sat down on the couch beside Harvey.

"How can you let her get away that?" Roxie asked Harvey.

"I don't like to argue with Morgan," Harvey said.

"You don't?" Roxie asked with surprise. Roxie liked to argue with everyone.

"No," Harvey told her.

"Why not?" Roxie demanded.

Now it was Harvey's turn to act surprised. "Have you seen Morgan when she's angry?" he asked. "I mean, she can get really scary."

Sabrina nodded. There was no debating that fact. "It's true," she said finally. "At least you know what costume you'll be wearing. I'm still deciding, and I've only got until tomorrow night!" She turned to Roxie. "How about you? You were about to tell me what you're wearing to the Halloween Howler when Hurricane Morgan blew in."

"I'm not going," Roxie replied simply.

"What!" Sabrina couldn't believe her ears.

"I said I'm not going," Roxie repeated.

"But the Halloween Howler is the biggest party of the year. Everyone will be there," Sabrina insisted.

"Everyone but me," Roxie told her. "Read my lips: There's no way I'm going to that party."

"Why not?" Sabrina asked.

"Look," Roxie said. "It's just that I'm tired of showing up for parties alone."

9

"But you won't be alone," Sabrina assured her. "We can go together."

Roxie sighed. "That's not exactly what I had in mind. I don't feel like going to another party without a date. I'm tired of standing against the wall hoping some sweaty frat freak will take pity on me and ask me to dance."

Sabrina stared at her roommate with amazement. On the outside Roxie seemed hard and prickly, like some sort of human cactus. But on the inside she was just as scared and insecure as anyone else. "I'm sure you can find a date. You know lots of guys," Sabrina said.

"Losers. Every one," Roxie countered. She turned to Harvey. "Present company excepted," she added.

"I think you'd better get out of here before this turns into a male-bashing fest," Sabrina warned Harvey.

Harvey shot Sabrina a grateful glance. He was more than happy to escape that fate. "Well, I'll see you guys later. I've got to go try on my tights."

"Come on, Roxie," Sabrina said as the door closed behind him. "You've gotta go to the party."

"Find me a guy who's interesting and who doesn't turn into an octopus with eight hands when it's time to kiss good night, and I'll consider it."

Sabrina thought about that. Who could she fix

Roxie up with? There was that guy Chuck in her journalism class. He was kind of cute, and very smart. And then there was that copy editor at the newspaper who'd just split with his girlfriend.

Sabrina stopped herself in mid thought. No. There was no way she was going to get involved with fixing Roxie up. The Spellmans weren't exactly known for their great judgment when it came to playing matchmaker. In fact, some of the matches her aunts had made had been disasters of the highest order. History-making matchup disasters! It was Sabrina's aunt Zelda who'd arranged that first blind date between Marc Antony and Cleopatra. The queen of the Nile was very taken with the handsome soldier. And at the time, Zelda was very proud of her accomplishments. But those two eventually managed to take the "till death us do part" thing a little too seriously. Who knew one little asp could cause so much trouble?

And then there was the time a few centuries later when Sabrina's aunt Hilda temporarily lost her mind and fixed Henry the VIII up with Anne Boleyn. Poor Anne. Being with a louse like Henry had caused her to lose a lot more than her mind: She'd lost her head as well!

That lack of matchmaking talent followed the Spellmans through the ages. At the last family reunion Sabrina heard a rumor that one of her cousins had had a hand in introducing Pamela Anderson and Tommy Lee. And everyone knows how that turned out.

Sabrina shook all thoughts of matchmaking from her head. There was no way she was going to risk Roxie being beheaded or having her picture plastered on the front page of the *National Enquirer*. Sabrina would have to find another way to convince Roxie to come to the party. "Come on," she begged. "You can't be alone that night. It's Halloween!"

"As far as I'm concerned it's simply October thirty-first," Roxie said. "Just another night."

Sabrina shook her head. "That's it!" she declared, grabbing Roxie's hand. "Come on! We're going on a field trip!"

Chapter 2

☆

"**D**eck the walls with spider eyes, fa la la la la, la la la la. Fill your belly with pumpkin pies, fa la la la la, la la la la," Sabrina sang through the mall an hour later while the girls were taking their Halloween field trip.

"Sabrina you're so bizarre," Roxie teased. "What's with the Halloween carols?"

Sabrina blushed. She hadn't realized she'd been singing out loud, and from the looks of the strangers around her, she'd been really belting it out. "I'm just trying to get you in the Halloween spirit," Sabrina told Roxie. "Isn't that why we came to the mall in the first place?"

"Oh, is that why?" Roxie asked. "I thought you were here to try out your new cabaret act."

"Very funny," Sabrina said. She held up a string

of bloodshot eyeballs. "Oooh, look! Blinking lights!"

Roxie rolled her eyes.

Sabrina frowned as she placed the eyeballs in her shopping basket. Roxie wasn't getting into the mood at all. In fact, this field trip to the mall seemed to be making her more depressed. Every time Roxie saw a couple holding hands, she looked as though she was going to puke.

"Get a room, will ya?" Roxie barked at a couple stealing a kiss in the Halloween costumes aisle of the store. The couple looked up, shocked, then darted off into the next aisle.

Roxie glanced at her watch and moaned quietly as she waited for Sabrina to pay for her Halloween decorations. It was taking a while. Besides the eyeball lights, Sabrina had picked out a glow-in-the-dark skeleton, a dancing goblin, a spider that said "Trick or Treat" when you pushed a button on its belly, six bags of candy corn, and a huge cardboard jack-o'-lantern with long, spindly legs.

"I hope you're not planning on putting those things all around the house," Roxie said.

Sabrina sighed. "That's what they're for."

"Can we go now?" Roxie moaned as Sabrina

gave the cashier a wad of bills and took her two shopping bags.

"There are still a lot of stores to check out," Sabrina said as the girls moved along past more shops—almost all of which were decorated in the appropriate black and orange. "Don't you just love the mall? Rain or shine, you can always shop."

Roxie shook her head. "This isn't exactly my scene. It's too mercenary. Too plastic." She looked at the price tag on a black macramé belt that was displayed in the window of a boutique. Seventy-five dollars! "Too expensive."

Sabrina was about to answer her, when something in the toy store window caught her eye. "Oh wow!" she exclaimed.

"What?" Roxie asked.

Sabrina pointed to a display of fashion dolls in the window. The dolls were all dressed up in tiny costumes, and holding miniature trick-or-treat bags. All the girl dolls had long, straight, thick hair— perfect for combing. The boy dolls had plastic helmet-head hair. A sign in the window said BETSY AND KURT. START YOUR CHILD ON THE ADVENTURE.

"I used to love my Betsy doll." Sabrina sighed, remembering. She turned to Roxie. "Did you have one?"

Roxie shot her a look. "You're kidding, right?"

"But you had a Malibu Barbie. You told me."

Roxie glared at Sabrina. "Does the word *secret* ring a bell?" she demanded. "Keep it down, would ya? Someone might hear you. Besides, Malibu Barbie was far cooler than those dolls."

"I had tons of Betsy dolls," Sabrina recalled. "Palm Beach Betsy, Ski Bunny Betsy, Mall Rat Betsy . . . oh, and of course I had Kurt, too."

"Kurt?" Roxie asked.

"Betsy's ever-faithful beau," Sabrina explained. "Don't you remember the commercial? 'Betsy's on the beach or in the snow. She's even in a fashion show. And everywhere Betsy goes, there's Kurt, her ever-faithful beau.'"

Roxie put her hand over Sabrina's mouth. "You're singing again," she hissed.

"Sorry," Sabrina apologized. "I just got carried away. When I was little, I loved Betsy and Kurt. They were the ultimate couple."

"Ever-faithful beau, yeah right," Roxie scoffed. "Only in the make-believe world of Betsy and friends."

"I wish you could meet someone like that," Sabrina said softly.

16

"What, plastic and empty-headed?"

"You know what I mean."

Roxie nodded. "I do," she said, softening. "But guys like that aren't real, Sabrina. Sooner or later every prince turns into a frog." Then, changing the subject, she asked, "Wanna get something to eat at the food court?"

But Sabrina was still staring at Betsy and Kurt. An idea was brewing in her head. "You go ahead," she told Roxie. "I'll meet you there. I just want to check something out in here."

Roxie shrugged. "Suit yourself. I'll go grab a table."

Sabrina hummed the Betsy jingle to herself as she made her way toward the doll section of the store. It was easy to find the Betsy section: Everything there was packaged in a pretty purple box. Betsy purple. There was no other purple exactly like it. Betsy purple was pale and glittery; little girls couldn't resist it. And just in case you weren't familiar with Betsy purple, every box in the aisle had the words OFFICIAL BETSY TOY stamped right on it. There were Betsy dolls, Betsy cars, Betsy town houses, Betsy kayaks, Betsy boats, and tons of Betsy clothes to buy. There were also stacks and stacks of Kurt dolls and clothes—an outfit for every possible occasion.

Sabrina reached up and took a Talking Hang Ten Kurt doll from the shelf. She smiled to herself. Kurt was exactly the way she remembered him from her childhood. He had the same close-mouthed smile and big brown eyes he'd always had. He was almost exactly the same—except he cost a lot more than when Sabrina was a little girl.

And this Kurt could do something Sabrina's childhood Kurt doll could never do: He could talk! The sticker on his box read, TALKING HANG TEN KURT SAYS TEN EXCITING PHRASES!

Wow! That settled it. Sabrina had to have Talking Hang Ten Kurt. He was just the gift Roxie needed to lift her spirits. Sabrina was so excited, she didn't even wait to hear his ten phrases.

"Come on, Kurt," Sabrina said as she carried the box to the front of the store. "Have I got a girl for you!"

Sabrina paid the cashier and hurried over to a quiet area of the mall where there were no stores and, consequently, no people. Quickly, Sabrina ripped the Kurt box open. Scraps of purple cardboard flew all over as Sabrina struggled with the metal ties and plastic hinges that kept Kurt in place during shipping.

Once Kurt was free from his little plastic shackles,

What a Doll!

Sabrina held up the doll and studied his face. A flood of memories came over her. She could see herself as a little girl wheeling Kurt and Betsy around in their purple plastic convertible. Sabrina remembered every outfit she'd ever dressed Kurt and Betsy in— their evening clothes, beach clothes, and ski outfits. And of course there were the times she took the dolls skinny-dipping in the tub at bathtime.

The Kurt that Sabrina held in her hands was dressed in a pair of long, orange shorts and a yellow-and-orange Hawaiian shirt. He wore brown loafers, but no socks on his feet. He looked like he was ready to hit the surf or sit beside Betsy at a cozy beach bonfire. There was an ad on the back of his box for Cowabunga surf wear and a swinging surfboard you could buy if you wanted to take Talking Hang Ten Kurt with you to the beach. Sabrina sighed, remembering how much she loved taking her Betsy and Kurt dolls to the beach. They looked so cute in their little bathing suits and tank tops.

But there was no time to marvel at Kurt's fashion sense right now. Roxie was waiting, and Sabrina had to get down to business. Quickly she looked around the secluded hallway. When she was absolutely certain no one was around, she sat the doll down on the floor.

"Roxie needs a hottie who'll treat her right.
A guy who'll be there day and night.
Someone to treat her as she deserves.
And really won't get on her nerves.
Kurt's got his own car, and a tux that's black.
He's a crush for Roxie who crushes back!
So hurry up and don't ask why.
Make this Kurt a real live guy."

Okay, so it wasn't exactly Shakespeare. But Sabrina was in a hurry. She wiggled her finger in the direction of the doll. A sudden flash of light filled the hall, and then a tall, dark, and slightly plastic-looking man appeared on the floor before her eyes. Sabrina stared at him in amazement. "Whoa! I didn't know you'd be this hot!" she exclaimed.

"Do you want to dance?" Kurt asked her.

Sabrina smiled. "Not now. We've got something more important to do. Let's hurry. Roxie's waiting at the food court. I really want her to meet you."

"Tennis anyone?" Kurt asked.

"Huh?"

"Betsy is the coolest!" Kurt exclaimed.

"Oh, I think you'll like Roxie even more than Betsy," Sabrina assured him. "She's great!"

20

"Let's go to the beach," Kurt said.

Sabrina shook her head. "We have to go meet Roxie," she told him.

"Want to share a soda?"

Sabrina sighed. "You can share one with Roxie. She likes soda."

"Tennis anyone?" Kurt asked.

Sabrina sighed. Talking Kurt was saying his ten exciting phrases in any random order. This could mean trouble. Talking in complete non-sequiturs was no big deal, as long as Kurt was talking to another doll. After all, it wasn't like Betsy was a brilliant conversationalist either. But Sabrina was pretty sure Roxie would notice that Kurt wasn't making any sense. And that was no good at all.

Sabrina thought about trying to fix this mess, but she wasn't sure what spell she could try to get Kurt to talk like any other guy. It was one thing to make a doll life-size; it was another to try to make him more human. That would be hard. And Sabrina had to get back to Roxie.

"Just try not to talk too much," Sabrina warned Kurt as she dragged him toward the food court.

"Purple is my favorite color," Kurt assured her.

Chapter 3

☆

As Sabrina walked through the mall toward the food court, she began to have second thoughts about introducing Roxie to a living doll. But it wasn't like she had too many other options. If Roxie didn't meet a loyal guy, she'd never go to the Halloween Howler—and she'd never understand how wonderful Halloween could really be. That would be a shame. Sabrina didn't want anyone, especially her best friend, to miss out on that!

Besides, it would be a total waste of a hunk if Roxie never got to meet Kurt!

As she entered the food court, Sabrina tried to convince herself that fixing Roxie up with a toy didn't actually count as matchmaking. Since Kurt wasn't real, if things started to go wacky, Sabrina would take care of it. She could always zap Kurt back to

Mini-Me size if he threatened to cut off her best friend's head.

"Where've you been?" Roxie asked as Sabrina approached the food court. Then she spotted Kurt walking stiffly a few inches behind Sabrina. "Oh, you've been busy," she added with more than a touch of ice in her tone.

"You mean with Kurt?" Sabrina asked Roxie.

"No, not with that dumb doll in the window," Roxie said. "I mean you've been busy with the guy standing next to you."

Sabrina smiled. Roxie obviously didn't notice that the guy standing next to her was the dumb doll in the window.

"Oh, this is such a funny coincidence." Sabrina laughed a little too hard. "His name is Kurt too."

Roxie managed a fake smile. "A regular riot," she said. She turned to Kurt. "Will you excuse us for a minute?" she asked as she pulled Sabrina by the elbow.

"What's up?" Sabrina asked.

"Some friend you are," Roxie hissed. "I thought we were here to cheer me up."

"We are," Sabrina assured her.

"And you plan on doing that by flaunting Mr. Tall, Dark, and Studly in my face?"

"Kurt's not a guy," Sabrina assured Roxie.

"Excuse me?"

"I mean he's not a guy I'd be interested in," Sabrina corrected herself. "He's an old friend. I've known him since I played with dolls." Sabrina breathed deeply. That was the truth . . . sort of. "Anyway, as soon as I ran into him in the toy store, I thought of you. I figured you two would hit it off."

"Well, he is kind of cute," Roxie admitted. "In a brawny, muscular sort of way. But what was he doing hanging out in a toy store? And why is he wearing shorts in October?"

"Oh, he was just hanging around by the toy store," Sabrina said. "He's kind of a little kid at heart. And as for the shorts, you know men have no fashion sense. Or clean clothes. That's probably the only outfit he had left."

"That reminds me," Roxie said. "I'm one pair of jeans away from wearing pajamas to class."

"Then you and Kurt will have a lot in common," Sabrina assured her. "Let's go hang with him."

Roxie shrugged. "There are worse ways to spend an afternoon, I guess."

"It'll be fine. Just go talk to the guy. You're gonna like him, I promise."

"Whatever," Roxie said doubtfully as she turned and headed back toward the table.

"Sorry about that," Roxie apologized to Kurt as she took a seat in the white metal chair across the table from him. "Girl stuff."

"Oh, you don't have to apologize to Kurt," Sabrina assured her as she plopped down beside him. "He doesn't care."

Roxie looked shocked. "Sabrina, what's with you?" she demanded. "This man has feelings. He's not made of plastic, you know."

"No, he's not. He's all flesh and bone. I swear," Sabrina agreed, a little too eagerly. She hurried to change the subject. "Anyway . . . Roxie, this is Kurt. Kurt, this is Roxie."

"Pleased to meet you." Roxie put out her hand. Kurt sat there, stone-faced. Shaking hands wasn't part of the Betsy doll world—mostly because the dolls' fingers didn't bend that way.

Embarrassed, Roxie pulled her hand back. "He doesn't say much, does he?" she whispered to Sabrina.

"Well, he . . . um . . . he can say lots of exciting things," Sabrina blurted out.

"Sure." Roxie didn't sound convinced. After a few more seconds of unnerving silence, she stood up. "Look, it was nice meeting you, Kurt, but I've got to get going to . . . uh . . . somewhere else."

Kurt smiled. "I love your hair!" he exclaimed.

Roxie sat back down. "Thanks."

"Purple is my favorite color," Kurt added.

Roxie knew her hair was dark brown. So Kurt had to be talking about her outfit. Her shirt was red. Her jeans were blue. No purple anywhere. "Is he color-blind?" she whispered to Sabrina.

"Um . . . yeah. Color-blind. That's it . . . yeah," Sabrina agreed.

"I love your hair," Kurt repeated.

Roxie smiled at Kurt. "I like your hair too. It's so shiny."

"Nothing like a coat of varnish to bring out the shine," Sabrina murmured under her breath.

"What?" Roxie asked.

"I said, 'Nothing like a good brush to bring out the shine,'" Sabrina said, covering for herself.

"Want to share a soda?" Kurt interrupted.

"Share a soda?" Roxie said. "What is he, cheap or something?" she whispered to Sabrina.

"He's just being cute. He's always been like that," Sabrina whispered back. She turned to Kurt. "I think we can each afford our own soda. Hey, I'll even treat. Come on, Kurt. You can help me get the sodas. Roxie, you stay here and save the table. Three sodas coming up."

Sabrina and Kurt walked toward the nearest soda counter. "Look, everything's going great here," she told him. "I think Roxie likes you. But you almost blew it with that 'Purple's my favorite color' thing," she warned. "You've got to stop talking."

Kurt nodded. "Let's party!" he said.

Sabrina rolled her eyes. "No partying. You have to keep quiet."

"Purple is my favorite color," Kurt answered.

Now Sabrina was getting annoyed. "If you don't stop talking, I'm going to take out your sound chip," she threatened.

Kurt got the message.

Sabrina turned to the clerk behind the counter. "Three sodas, please."

Sabrina and Kurt carried the sodas back to the table. For a while, everyone sipped in silence. Finally, it was Roxie who tried to start a conversation. "So Kurt, are you from around here, or somewhere far away?"

"He was made in the U.S.A.," Sabrina assured her.

"I figured that," Roxie replied. "What was I

supposed to think—he was made in China? What I meant was, was he brought up in the Boston area?"

"Uh, yeah," Sabrina answered sheepishly. "He's from around here. I told you, we played together when I was a kid."

Roxie smiled at Kurt. Kurt smiled back.

"So, what do you say we walk around a little more?" Sabrina suggested as she took the last sip of her soda.

"Sounds good to me," Roxie agreed. "How about you, Kurt?"

Kurt opened his mouth to speak, but shut it again when he saw the warning look in Sabrina's eyes. He nodded instead.

"Good, " Sabrina said. "I'll just throw these cups out, and we can shop."

"I'll help you," Roxie volunteered. She leaped up from her seat and walked over to the trash can with Sabrina. Time for more girl talk.

"So, what do you think?" Sabrina whispered.

"Is he really a nice guy?" Roxie wondered. "I mean, he hasn't said anything to make me think otherwise, but . . ." She paused for a moment. "Come to think of it, he hasn't said much at all."

"Oh, he's that strong, silent type," Sabrina assured her.

"He does look pretty strong," Roxie agreed. "Did you see the muscles bulging out of his shirt?"

"And he's a nice guy. Really loyal," Sabrina assured her.

"What about his octopus tendencies?" Roxie asked.

"His what?"

"You know, is he the kind of guy who's all hands at the end of the night?"

Sabrina laughed. "I doubt it. I've known him forever and he's never even tried to kiss me."

"Well, there has to be something wrong with him somewhere," Roxie said. "Nobody's that perfect."

Sabrina sighed. "Look, no one's asking you to marry the guy. I just thought you might want to ask him to the Halloween party."

"You think he'd want to go?"

"You'll never know unless you ask him," Sabrina said.

Roxie nodded. She looked over at where Kurt was sitting, staring into space. She smiled at him and waved. He smiled back. "Okay," she said as she walked back to the table. "Here goes nothing."

Sabrina stood to the side and watched as her tough-girl roommate turned to a stressed-out bundle of jelly. Amazing.

"So, um, Kurt," Roxie said as she walked over toward the table where Kurt was sitting all by himself. She blushed slightly as she attempted to avoid Sabrina's not-too-subtle stares from across the room. "There's this party on Halloween. It's at one of the frats on campus. Anyway, I'm sure you already have plans, but if you don't, maybe you and I could—"

"Let's party!" Kurt exclaimed before she could even finish her sentence.

"Oh hey, so you want to go with me?" Roxie asked, barely hiding her disbelief.

"I'll pick you up in my car," Kurt continued.

"Your car?" Roxie said excitedly. "You have a car? Wow. What kind is it?"

"Purple is my favorite color," Kurt said.

"A purple car?" Roxie said curiously. "Well, whatever you're into."

"Let's go for pizza," Kurt suggested.

Roxie shook her head. "Thanks, but I'm not really hungry. "

"Let's party!" Kurt exclaimed

Roxie smiled. "I love your attitude. I can't wait either."

Sabrina grinned as she saw Roxie visibly relax.

She figured that was her cue to return to the table. "So what's up?" she asked as she reached Kurt and Roxie.

"Kurt's coming to the Sigma Kappa Delta Halloween Howler tomorrow," Roxie said.

"Is he going alone?" Sabrina teased.

"Funny," Roxie snapped. "As a matter of fact, he's picking me up in his car."

"His car?" Sabrina asked. "What car? He doesn't have a car."

"Sure he does," Roxie said. "Don't you, Kurt?"

Kurt nodded.

"He has a purple car. He told me," Roxie insisted. "Most of the guys I date don't even have enough money for a bicycle, never mind a car!"

Sabrina glared at Kurt. "You told her you had a car?"

"Oh, it's okay, Sabrina. He wasn't bragging or anything," Roxie assured her. "It just came up in conversation."

"Gee," Sabrina said. "I'm sorry I missed that conversation."

"So, where do you want to go next?" Roxie asked. "Do you think we need a few more Halloween decorations? Maybe some candy for the trick-or-treaters? I think I saw a sale on Chocolate Chewies at the candy store on the second floor."

Roxie was definitely filled with the Halloween spirit. There was just the trace of an uncharacteristic bounce in her step as she raced off in the direction of the candy store.

Sabrina glared at Kurt. "I'll zap you up a car. But that's it. From now on, keep quiet, you understand?" she hissed.

Kurt nodded. "Tennis anyone?" he asked.

Roxie may have been psyched for the Halloween Howler, but Harvey sure wasn't. He was still moping and holding his blue tights when he returned to Sabrina's college house that afternoon.

None of the roommates was home, but the front door was unlocked, so Harvey let himself in and sat down quietly on the couch. He held up the tights and stared at them for the billionth time that day. "How could she make me do this?" he moaned. "I don't believe it!"

"Oh, I'd believe anything when it comes to Morgan," a man's voice bellowed from the kitchen windowsill. "You would, too, if you'd been around women as long as I have."

Harvey turned around. No one was in the room, other than Sabrina's cat, Salem.

"Oh hi, Salem," Harvey said. "I didn't notice you."

"Obviously," the cat agreed. "You didn't even say hello. I'll try not to be too insulted."

Most people would be surprised to be greeted by a talking cat, but Harvey wasn't the least bit shocked. Oh sure, there'd been a time when Harvey would've been totally freaked by the idea of having a conversation with a cat, but that was before he'd figured out Sabrina's secret. Harvey was the only one of her mortal friends who knew Sabrina was a witch. After years of being zapped into fairy tales, turned into various creatures, and spending time in what seemed like another realm, he'd pieced the puzzle together. It had happened because Sabrina had finally exhausted the allotment of mind-erasing spells she could use on Harvey. At just about the time he and Sabrina graduated from high school, Harvey had learned about Sabrina's magic. It explained a lot about the previous four years. And now that he knew, a talking cat wasn't all that weird to him anymore.

Of course, Salem wasn't actually a cat. Despite

the fact that he had four paws, was covered in black fur, and liked cleaning himself with his tongue, Salem was actually a witch. Or at least he had been.

Salem Saberhagen had been sentenced by the Witches' Council to one hundred years as a familiar—a witch in a cat's body—after he'd been caught trying to take over the world.

Salem may have gained a fur coat, lost his thumbs, and developed a craving for sardines, but there were still parts of his old self that remained intact—like his voice and his love of money and power.

"So what'd Morgan make you do this time?" Salem asked Harvey.

"She's making me dress as her Romeo at the Halloween Howler." Harvey held up the blue tights so Salem could see them. "I have to wear these to a frat party."

"Personally, I don't think you guys have the legs to carry it off," Salem teased.

"Very funny," Harvey moaned.

Salem leaped off the windowsill and padded his way over to Harvey.

"If you don't want to go as Romeo, why don't you just tell Morgan you've changed your mind?"

Harvey shook his head. "You don't tell Morgan things. She tells you."

Salem cocked his little black head curiously. "Is that a law?"

Harvey frowned. "It's a law of self-preservation. Morgan'll kill me if I disappoint her."

Salem licked his paws casually. "I think I can help you, Harvey . . . that is, if you want my help."

Harvey looked from Salem to the tights and back again. The guy was desperate. He'd take help from anyone—even a talking cat who most certainly had an ulterior motive. "Yes!" he begged. "Please."

Salem turned his back to Harvey. "Scratch, will you?" he asked. "Right between my shoulder bones."

Harvey scratched.

"Oh, that's good." Salem wiggled his back a little.

"Salem," Harvey said, sounding more than a little annoyed, "about that help?"

"Oh yeah. Harvey, you need to be more like me. More independent, more cunning, more"—Salem peeked over his shoulder at Harvey's unbrushed hair and coffee-stained T-shirt—"more well groomed. What you need is Cattitude."

Harvey looked confused. "What's Cattitude?"

Salem rolled his eyes. "Cattitude. Cat-Attitude, get it?"

"I didn't know that was a word."

Salem smiled proudly—well, at least as a cat could smile. "It wasn't . . . until I made it up."

"Oh," Harvey said. "So it isn't real."

"Cattitude is very real, Harvey, and don't you forget it. I can teach you how to develop it. Before long, you'll have Morgan scratching you behind the ears whenever you demand it."

"Why would I want her to do that?"

Salem sighed. This wasn't going to be easy. "It's a metaphor, Harvey. Anyway, I've developed this amazing Cattitude course—guaranteed to make you self-confident and assertive. It's all in my new, easy-to-follow program. And it can be yours for one hundred dollars . . . plus shipping and handling, of course."

Harvey moaned slightly. "I guess I'll have to wear the tights, then."

"Haven't you been listening?" Salem demanded. "I said I can help you."

"I know," Harvey assured him. "But I don't have one hundred dollars. I used to date Morgan, remember? I'm still paying off the bills."

Salem didn't seem surprised by Harvey's financial situation. In fact, he'd been counting on it. "Well, maybe we can come up with another way for you to pay me," Salem suggested slyly, "seeing as you're a friend of the family."

Harvey sat up at attention. "How?" he asked. "I'll do anything. I can't wear these to a frat party. I really need Cattitude."

"Lots of people need Cattitude. And you can help me get it to them. I need you to go on TV and do an infomercial for Cattitude. And I'll also need you to star in a how-to videotape. "

"Me?"

Salem nodded. "I'd do it myself, but I think the idea of a talking cat might not be taken seriously. I need a human to be my representative in the market-place."

"But why me?" Harvey asked. "I have absolutely no Cattitude."

"I know," Salem said. "You're more like a mouse than a cat."

"Thanks a lot," Harvey replied sarcastically.

"But that's the point," Salem said. "I can change you. And if you can change, anyone can. You're the perfect before-and-after example."

"Wow!" Harvey exclaimed. "No one's ever called me perfect before—except my mother, and I don't think that counts."

Salem ignored him. "Besides, you're the only mortal I can actually speak to," he continued. "So, do we have a deal?"

Harvey picked up Salem's paw and shook it. "It's a deal," he agreed.

"Good," Salem said. "Come on back to Hilda and Zelda's with me. I've got a video camera all set up. We can film the infomercial this afternoon and have it on the air by tonight. Don't ya just love modern technology?" The cat reached over and scratched at the blue tights. A huge run appeared across the knee.

"Oh no!" Harvey shouted. "What did you do? You wrecked them. Morgan's gonna kill me!"

Salem took a deep breath. This was going to be more work than he'd thought.

Salem wasn't the only one who was working hard to get his plan moving. Sabrina had her hands full with Kurt. As soon as Roxie left the mall to go to a late-afternoon class, Sabrina dragged him into the parking lot. She was going to have to conjure up a car for him . . . a purple car! And making up a spell for a purple car was no easy task—nothing rhymes with "purple"!

"Kurt needs to travel, but not very far, so I'm giving him the purple car!" she said finally. It wasn't very original, but at least it rhymed!

With a single wiggle of her index finger, Sabrina whipped up a purple sports car with plush leather seats and a five-disc CD player in the dashboard. Hey, why not? It didn't cost anything, and Sabrina figured Roxie may as well show up at the party in style.

"Okay, let's take this baby for a spin," Sabrina said as she hopped into the passenger seat.

Kurt sat down behind the wheel. He didn't move.

"Come on, let's go," Sabrina told him.

But Kurt just stared at the car dashboard.

"Oh, maybe you can't drive a shift," Sabrina said. "No prob." She wiggled her finger and switched the car to automatic.

But Kurt still didn't seem to know what to do. "Betsy is the coolest," he mumbled, sounding confused. "Do you want to dance?"

Sabrina was worried now. Kurt didn't seem to know how to drive. But he'd promised Roxie he'd pick her up in his car tomorrow night. How was

Sabrina going to explain this without Roxie thinking she'd fixed her up with another lying loser?

"Tennis anyone?" Kurt said sadly. He could tell Sabrina was disappointed in him.

"Shhhh," Sabrina said. "I'm trying to think." Frantically, Sabrina searched her brain for a solution to her problem.

"I'll pick you up in my car," Kurt said.

Sabrina grinned. That was it! Kurt would have to pick Roxie up in his car. A Kurt car! Apparently Kurt was only comfortable in things from his own line of toys. It must have been something Sabrina had said when she'd cast her spell on the doll. Probably that line about having his own car and his own tux.

Sabrina really had to be more careful when it came to casting spells. But it was too late to think about that now. She'd have to buy Kurt his own car. "Come on," Sabrina said. "We need to go back to that toy store."

"Let's go to the beach," Kurt replied.

"No, we have to . . . oh, never mind," Sabrina said as she dragged Kurt back into the mall.

Chapter 4

☆

As Sabrina and Kurt stood outside her college house, she looked around. Sabrina had to be absolutely sure no one was looking. When she was certain the street was empty, she unwrapped the plastic purple convertible Kurt had picked out from the Betsy doll collection and set it on the ground.

The car had been very expensive—almost fifty dollars! That seemed an awful lot of money for a couple of pieces of painted plastic with wheels. But it was the only car Sabrina was certain Kurt could drive. She'd had no choice.

Zap! With one wiggle of her index finger, the overpriced kiddie convertible went from miniature to full-size.

Kurt's eyes brightened when he saw his trusty convertible standing there before him. He walked

41

over and lovingly ran his hand over the purple plastic hood. Sabrina giggled. She remembered that old rhyme her aunt Hilda loved: "The difference between men and boys is the size of their toys."

That statement was never more true than right now!

Sabrina gently pulled Kurt away from the car. "You can drive it later," she assured him. "Let's go inside now."

"Let's go for pizza," Kurt said.

Sabrina shook her head. "We can order in. Right now, we're going to see Roxie. You remember Roxie, right?"

"I love your hair," Kurt replied.

"Oh thanks. I just tried a new conditioner and . . ." Sabrina stopped herself, remembering that Kurt's responses were totally random. "Save it for Roxie," she told him.

Sabrina opened the door to the house and looked around. There was no one in the living room. But Sabrina had no doubts that Roxie was home. She could hear the loud, head-banging music coming from the stereo in the bedroom the two girls shared.

"Hey Rox, I've got a surprise for you," Sabrina shouted over the din.

There was no answer.

"ROXIE!" Sabrina shouted louder.

Again, no answer.

"Wait here," Sabrina told Kurt. Then she headed into the bedroom and turned off the stereo.

Roxie, who had been sitting on her bed reading, looked up in surprise. "Hey, what'd you do that for?"

Sabrina shook her head. "How can you study with the music turned up so loud?"

"It wasn't loud," Roxie said. She reached up and tightened the ponytail on top of her head.

Sabrina figured Roxie must have been doing some heavy studying. Whenever she really wanted to concentrate, Roxie piled her dark hair on top of her head.

"They could hear the stereo in Peru," Sabrina assured her.

"It's just mood music," Roxie replied.

"Bad mood music," Sabrina countered.

"Hey, Spellman, if you don't like my music just say so . . . ," Roxie said, a threatening tone taking over her voice.

Sabrina knew when to change the subject.

"Anyway, I've got a surprise out there for you," she said. "Guess who's here to see you?"

"Who?"

"Kurt."

Roxie's eyes looked shocked. "He's here?"

Sabrina grinned. "In the flesh." Well, sort of.

"I thought I'd just see him tomorrow." Roxie seemed astonished.

"That's Kurt. When he likes someone, he showers them with attention," Sabrina assured her. "Come on out, he's waiting."

"Wait a minute," Roxie said. She ran over to the mirror and pulled the scrunchy from her hair. Then she began brushing her long dark locks.

"What are you doing?" Sabrina asked. Roxie never fixed her hair for company.

"He said he liked my hair, remember?" she reminded Sabrina.

Sabrina choked back a laugh. If Roxie only knew how many times a day that random phrase was emitted from Kurt's sound chip. "You look fine," Sabrina assured her.

Roxie took one last look at herself in the mirror and then hurried into the living room. Sabrina followed close behind. She knew better than to leave

Kurt and Roxie alone. There was no telling what he might do or say.

"I love your hair," Kurt said as Roxie entered the room.

Roxie shot Sabrina an I-told-you-so look. "Thanks," she said. "Can I get you something? A soda, maybe?"

"I love your hair," Kurt said again.

Sabrina gulped. That was the third time in a row Kurt had said that. "He really knows how to compliment a girl, don't you think, Rox?" she said quickly, covering.

"Well, he's got a thing for hair, anyway," Roxie said with a shrug. She reached into the refrigerator and pulled out three cans of soda. When she turned around, Kurt was standing right in front of her. Roxie handed him a soda.

"Do you want to dance?" Kurt asked.

Roxie looked at him strangely. "What did you say?"

Sabrina laughed. "You're so funny, Kurt," she said quickly. "This guy's always ready for a party."

"Let's party," Kurt added.

Roxie nodded. "You're right, we probably should talk about the party. We have to go in costume. Do you have any ideas? I mean, we don't have to wear costumes that work as a couple, but I figured as long as we were going to the party together . . . well . . ."

"Let's go to the beach!" Kurt blurted out.

"The beach?" Roxie asked. "Now? It's October in Massachusetts. A little cold for the surf, don't you think?"

"I think Kurt means you could go as surfers to the Halloween Howler," Sabrina butted in quickly. "Isn't that what you meant, Kurt?"

Kurt didn't answer. He was busy staring out the window at his purple convertible.

"What a great idea!" Roxie said. "We could wear beach clothes and carry surfboards around. We can even get some fake surfer tattoos put on for the night." She turned to Sabrina. "You know, maybe there *is* something to this Halloween thing. Have you decided what costume you're going to buy?"

Sabrina sighed. She doubted she'd be able to spend very much on her own costume. She'd just blown fifty bucks on a plastic purple car. "I haven't really had a chance to think about my costume," Sabrina told her.

"Maybe Kurt can come up with an idea for you, too," Roxie suggested. "He seems pretty good at that kind of thing." She turned to Kurt. "Any ideas for Sabrina's costume?"

"Betsy is the coolest," he replied.

Sabrina gulped. She'd promised Roxie that Kurt was loyal. Now here he was planning to go to a party with her *and* talking about his old girlfriend at the same time.

But Roxie didn't seem upset at all. In fact, just the opposite was true. "Oh! Great idea!" Roxie exclaimed. "Sabrina, you were obsessed with that dumb doll today. Maybe you should go as a Betsy doll to the party."

Sabrina shook her head no. The last thing she wanted to go to the party as was Betsy. She could only deal with one doll at a time.

Chapter 5

"**S**abrina! you've got to see this. Get up and get out here!"

Roxie's shouts pulled Sabrina right out of her dream—a very good dream, in fact. One involving Brad Pitt and a deserted island. Sabrina was going to make her pay for that!

"What do you want?" Sabrina's voice sounded groggy. But that wasn't unusual; groggy was exactly how she always sounded at 3:00 in the morning. Even 3:00 on Halloween morning.

"You've got to see this!" Roxie shouted, yanking the covers from Sabrina's bed. "Harvey's on TV!"

"He's what?" Suddenly Sabrina was wide awake. "Why would Harvey be on TV?"

"He's doing an infomercial."

"A what?"

48

"An infomercial," Roxie repeated. "You know, one of those hour-long TV ads. He's selling something called Cattitude. Kurt and I were sitting on the couch channel surfing and we saw Harvey on the TV. Come on, you're missing it!"

Sabrina got out of bed and threw on her robe. Then she looked around for her slippers. "What are you and Kurt doing watching infomercials at three o'clock in the morning?" she asked.

"Boy, is Kurt a night owl. He doesn't seem like he's ever going to close his eyes. I don't even think he blinks!"

"Oh, he can blink," Sabrina murmured sleepily as she searched under her bed. "It said so on the box."

"What?" Roxie asked.

"I said he always had the latest bedtime on my aunts' block," Sabrina said.

"Well, he's still like that. And he loves TV." Roxie peeked out into the living room. "He's still sitting there, in the exact same position, staring at the screen."

"I just have to find my slippers," Sabrina murmured.

"Forget the slippers," Roxie urged. "You gotta see this."

Sabrina trudged out into the living room behind Roxie. The light of the TV flickered in the darkness.

"You two were watching TV in the dark, huh?" Sabrina teased. "Nice."

"It was completely innocent," Roxie said. "Kurt has been a total gentleman. Unfortunately."

"Hey, isn't that what you wanted—a guy who's not an octopus at the end of the night?" Sabrina whispered.

"Okay, but it wouldn't hurt him to be a little like a squid."

Sabrina walked over to the couch, sat down beside Kurt, and focused her attention on the TV. Sure enough, there was Harvey—dressed in a black suit and tie. His hair was slicked back, and it looked like he'd grown a thin, whiskerlike mustache. Sabrina was pretty sure he must have drawn it on for TV. Harvey had never had a mustache before. He appeared impeccably groomed.

"Cattitude can change your life. Just look at what it did for me . . . the Cattitude Dude."

Home movies of Harvey appeared on the screen. Sabrina smiled. This was the high school Harvey she remembered so well. There was Harvey tripping over his shoelace as he leaped up to catch a football. Next there was a shot of Harvey banging his head against an open locker. There was an audio clip of Morgan ordering Harvey to take her to a fancy restaurant (which had to have come from Harvey's answering machine tape). Finally there was a video clip of Harvey walking down the street in a jacket from his father's exterminating business—the coat had a big dead bug embroidered on the back of it.

Then the camera returned to the all-new Harvey—the Cattitude Dude. "Look at me now," Harvey said. "I'm suave and sophisticated. I'm graceful as a cat." Harvey walked across the infomercial set as gracefully as a fashion model on a . . . well, a catwalk, for lack of a better term. He smiled at the camera. "And I do what I want, when I want. . . . No one is going to tell me to wear tights when I don't want to."

Sabrina gulped. Morgan was going to have a cow when she heard that Harvey had defied her on television!

"Oh, and I eat better now, too. A healthy body and a healthy mind are all part of the Cattitude program. I'd rather have a sardine than a chocolate bar any day." Harvey put a forkful of sardines in his mouth and chewed.

If Sabrina wasn't mistaken, she could swear she heard him purr ever so slightly.

"Wow, look at him," Roxie said. "I can't believe that's Harvey. He looks so sophisticated."

Sabrina had to admit that Harvey seemed more confident. But she kind of liked the old, unsophisticated Harvey.

"This purr-fect plan can change your life too. Just call the number on your screen. For a mere one hundred dollars you'll be able to master the Cattitude attitude in no time."

Harvey bent down and picked up a small black cat. "We can all learn from the master."

"Where did Harvey get the idea for this?" Roxie wondered.

Sabrina's eyes narrowed. "Salem!" she exclaimed.

"Oh come on, Sabrina, it's just a black cat. It could be any cat," Roxie told her.

"No, it's Salem all right," Sabrina told her.

"How do you know?"

Sabrina sighed. There was no way she could explain to Roxie that Salem was quite possibly the only cat in the world who could cook up a scheme like this!

"Well, I'm zonked," Roxie said finally. "I'm going to leave you two old friends to watch infomercials together."

"Tennis anyone?" Kurt blurted out suddenly.

Roxie laughed. "You're such a riot!" she exclaimed as she went into her room to crash.

Sabrina took Kurt by the hand. "Come on," she said. "We're going to my aunts' house. You'll be safer there."

"I'll pick you up in my car," Kurt said.

"No. I know a faster way," Sabrina assured him. She waved her finger in the air. In a flash, they arrived at Hilda and Zelda's house.

"Okay, you're going to stay in my old room," Sabrina said as she dragged Kurt up the stairs. "And I don't want you to leave for any reason. Tomorrow we'll go to the toy store and get you your costume."

"Do you want to dance?" Kurt asked.

Sabrina sighed. "Save it for the Halloween Howler."

Sabrina opened the door to her room. "We're here," she whispered to Kurt. "Now keep quiet. The fewer people who know you're here, the better."

Kurt sat down on the bed. Suddenly, a loud, pained screech filled the room.

"Watch the tail!" Salem shouted.

Sabrina flicked on the light. "Sorry, Salem. We didn't know you were here."

Salem eyed Sabrina and Kurt suspiciously. "Apparently. Who's the new guy?"

Sabrina turned beet red. "Salem! You don't think he and I . . . I mean, I wouldn't bring a real guy here."

"What is he? A fake guy?" Salem asked.

"Exactly," Sabrina said.

"Works for me, but I don't think your aunts will buy it."

Sabrina sighed. "He's not real. He's a doll. I just gave him the gift of life for a little while."

"Any particular reason, Dr. Frankenstein?"

"Roxie said there weren't any great guys who were loyal and true. And I saw the Kurt doll in the window, and I remembered the song . . . 'Betsy's on the beach or in the snow. She's even in a fashion show. And everywhere Betsy goes, there's Kurt, her ever-faithful beau.'"

Salem put his paws over his ears. "Please, not the singing," he moaned. "Anything but the singing."

"Oh, never mind." Sabrina scowled. "And you've got a few questions to answer yourself, Mr. Cattitude."

Salem perked up. "You saw the infomercial?" he asked excitedly.

"Oh yeah," Sabrina replied. "How'd you manage to dupe Harvey into being your front man?"

"Harvey's middle name is Dupe," Salem joked. "But, I didn't even need to trick him. I just convinced him that he could stand up to Morgan if he were a little more like me."

"The one thing the world doesn't need is more of you," Sabrina told him.

"Well, plenty of people disagree with you. We got 1,473 orders tonight. I've got to increase my order at the manufacturer first thing in the morning. And we're going to run that infomercial three times a day for the next week," Salem boasted.

Sabrina did some quick math. 1,473 times 100 dollars. "That's almost one hundred and fifty thousand dollars!" Sabrina exclaimed in a voice that was both surprised and a little impressed. Then she stopped and eyed Salem suspiciously. "What does Harvey get out of this?"

"The honor of being my spokeshuman . . . and a free Cattitude course," Salem replied as he groomed his paws with his tongue.

"Some honor," Sabrina scolded. "You're cheating him."

"I think it's a very good deal. Harvey needs me. He turns into a little mouse around Morgan. I'm giving him his independence."

It was hard to argue with logic like that, and Sabrina knew it. The truth was, if Cattitude really worked, Harvey would be free of Morgan. But on the other hand . . .

"What if Cattitude makes Harvey a joke on campus? Then he'll be worse off than when he started . . . which is what usually happens when you meddle in people's lives, Salem."

Sabrina sighed. She turned to Kurt. "Stay here, and keep out of trouble," she told the doll. "I'm going to sack out on the couch for a little while. I'll come back for you later."

"Betsy is the coolest," Kurt told her.

"Not as cool as Roxie, right?" Sabrina reminded him.

"I love your hair," Kurt responded.

"Whatever." Sabrina looked at Kurt. His once neat, beach party outfit now seemed wrinkled and messy. "Time for a quick change," she said as she wiggled her finger.

There was a flash of light. Sabrina stood back to admire her work. But there was Kurt, sitting on her bed, wearing the exact same clothes. Something had gone wrong.

Once again, Sabrina wiggled her finger. And once again, the light flashed in her room. But Kurt was still in his beachwear.

Sabrina remembered what had happened with Kurt's car. He'd only been able to drive a genuine Betsy doll accessory. Which meant those were the only clothes he could wear.

Suddenly Sabrina remembered something she hadn't thought about in years. "I hope it's still here," she muttered to herself as she dragged the desk chair over to her old closet. Quickly, she climbed on the chair and reached high until she could get the small purple plastic carrying case that sat on the top shelf.

Inside the case was another of Sabrina's big secrets—maybe not as big as being a witch, but definitely something she didn't want her friends to know about

Sabrina still had her favorite Betsy doll.

Not that she played with her Snowbunny Betsy or anything. She just sort of kept her around. Sometimes she looked at her . . . and changed her clothes or fixed her hair. But just once in a while.

Sabrina quickly rifled through her Betsy carrying case for some old Kurt clothes. But she hadn't saved any of those. All she had were Betsy dresses, bikinis, and . . . a single pair of purple pajamas. They were pretty ratty and wrinkled, but they would have to do.

With a wiggle of her finger, Sabrina zapped them onto Kurt.

No doubt about it. Sabrina was going to have to go to the toy store after class and pick up a few outfits for Kurt.

That was going to cost her.

Sabrina frowned and made a mental note to herself: *No more being creative when I make up spells.* Her cute little rhyme about Kurt having his own clothes and accessories was running up her credit card bill big-time! But what could she do? "Salem, make sure Kurt doesn't go anywhere," she told the cat.

"What's in it for me?" Salem hissed back.

"You watch Kurt, and I don't pull the plug on your little Cattitude scheme," Sabrina said firmly. "Aunt Zelda and Aunt Hilda don't have any idea about this, do they?"

Salem thought about all the cartons of Cattitude tapes and DVDs already being manufactured. He'd had to lay out the cash in advance, and he couldn't get his money back now. If Sabrina told Zelda and Hilda about Cattitude, guaranteed they'd put the kibosh on his latest business venture. They were real party poopers.

And if Hilda and Zelda put an end to Cattitude,

Salem would be out a bundle of cash. He frowned. "You drive a hard bargain, blondie," he said to Sabrina.

Sabrina smiled knowingly at the cat. "I learned from the best."

Salem couldn't argue with that. And unfortunately, she'd learned her lessons well. "Deal," he said finally. I'll make sure plastic man stays put."

Sabrina grinned. "That's what I thought you'd say." She turned to Kurt. "Don't you go anywhere."

Kurt looked at the pajamas he was wearing. "Purple is my favorite color."

59

Chapter 6

☆

Rolling off the couch at 7:30 A.M. was painful after a night of Kurt-sitting, but Sabrina couldn't miss her English lit class. It was just a few weeks until midterms.

Besides, Sabrina wanted to make sure she was there for Harvey if he needed her. Despite Salem's assurances, Sabrina had a feeling that if anyone at his school or hers had seen that Cattitude infomercial, he was going to be getting some major grief. She knew he was auditing a class at Adams this morning, and she wanted to catch him before it started. But she was too late.

Sure enough, as soon as Sabrina walked onto the campus green she found Harvey surrounded by a huge group of college students. They were all laughing really hard.

Poor Harvey. What a way to spend Halloween.

"That cat is going to be down to eight lives when I see him," Sabrina muttered to herself. Quickly she hurried over to Harvey. He needed her.

"Hi, Harvey," Sabrina said as she fought her way through the crowd of giggling students. "Don't you have to get to class?"

"Oh don't go, Harvey," a pretty girl with long brown braids begged. "We were just getting started."

"Come on, that's enough," Sabrina argued. "Leave the guy alone."

"But he was just telling us a cat joke," a huge football player type groaned. "I want to hear the punch line."

"Harvey's not a punch line!" Sabrina declared.

"I never said he was," the big guy said. "I said I wanted to hear *the* punch line."

Harvey looked over at Sabrina and gently stroked the few whiskerlike hairs below his nose. "It's okay, Sabrina, these are just a few fans."

"Fans?" Sabrina asked.

"Did you happen to turn on the TV last night?" Harvey asked.

"Yes. And that's why I'm here. I thought you could use my help," she answered.

Harvey let out a small laugh that was almost like a purr. "I don't need any help. Cattitude is all about self-reliance. As long as someone cleans the litter box, a Cattitude Dude can handle anything."

Sabrina looked at him oddly. "Cleans the litter box?"

Harvey sighed. "It's a metaphor," he told her. "Let someone else clean up the mess. That's what cats do, and it works for them. "

Before Sabrina could respond, a few members of the swim team, easily identifiable by their shaved heads and broad shoulders, began applauding wildly, and cheering Harvey with a shout that could only be identified as a catcall.

"Go Harvey! Go Harvey!" the crowd chanted.

"Thank you," Harvey said. "But it isn't me you should be cheering. It's Cattitude. Anybody can have it. All you have to do is call 1-800-555-CATS and order your Cattitude tape or DVD."

Instantly, a sea of cell phones popped up in the crowd.

"What's that number again?" one girl shouted out.

"1-800-555-CATS," Harvey reminded her.

"Oh Harvey, there you are," Morgan's voice rang out above the crowd of kids ordering their Cattitude packages. "I've been looking for you all over."

For once, no one seemed to notice the campus queen. They were too busy dialing.

"Move over, I need to talk to Harvey," Morgan demanded as she pushed her way through the crowd.

The crowd grew quiet and stepped aside. Everyone on campus knew not to cross Morgan when she gave a direct order.

Morgan sashayed triumphantly up to Harvey. "So, have you tried on your costume yet? I was pretty sure it was your size. And don't worry about the ripped blue tights."

"How did you know about the rip in the tights?" Harvey asked suspiciously.

"I found them in the trash this morning," Morgan explained. "Don't worry. I can get you a new pair. Oh, and I almost forgot to tell you— I ordered your wig last night. It's long and curly."

The crowd gasped. Many of them hung up their phones as they tried to picture the Cattitude Dude in tights. It was not a pretty picture.

"Oh man!" One of the swimmers exclaimed. "I thought you were a superhero. I guess you're just Catwoman!"

The crowd laughed. But this time they weren't laughing with Harvey; they were laughing at him. The tide had turned.

But not for long. Harvey smiled at the crowd. He nonchalantly lifted his hand to groom his hair. When he was satisfied that he was purr-fectly coiffed, he smiled at Morgan. "Don't worry about the tights, or the wig, or anything else. I'm not going to the party with you. You'll have to find yourself another Romeo."

Morgan looked as though someone had slapped her across the face. "You've made a big mistake, Harvey Kinkle," she declared.

All eyes were on Harvey. No one had ever had the guts to stand up to Morgan before. This was the ultimate test. And it wasn't clear whether Harvey was going to pass. For a moment, he seemed to be struggling with himself. Would he be able to stand up to Morgan? Was he a cat or a mouse?

Finally, Harvey spoke. "Yes, I have," he told Morgan sincerely.

The crowd started to move away. Cattitude was obviously a fake.

Or was it?

"I've hurt your feelings. And I'm sorry for that,

but you'll have to adjust. I am not going to the party dressed as Romeo."

The crowd turned back and listened.

"I don't need to be your Romeo. I don't need your version of popular. The only person I need to feel popular with is me . . . and the thousands of satisfied Cattitude customers I've inspired," Harvey concluded as he beamed with inner Cattitude.

"Woo-hoo!" Sabrina cheered. Even she was caught up in the beauty of the moment.

"Go Harvey! Go Harvey!" the crowd chanted.

"Catti-what?" Morgan demanded.

But Harvey didn't answer. He couldn't hear her over the roar of the crowd.

"Excuse me, I was speaking," Morgan said firmly.

"Could you move?" A tall girl with curly brown ringlets tapped Morgan on the shoulder. "You're blocking my view of Harvey."

Morgan shot the girl her most venomous look. "Pardon me?" she said. "Did you actually ask me to move? That's my line, hon."

The girl frowned. "If you want an autograph, you'll have to get behind me. I was here first."

Morgan looked at her in disbelief. "An autograph? Why would I want an autograph? I dated the guy for months. I've seen his signature a lot of times. Mostly on credit card bills in some of the most exclusive restaurants . . . which I introduced him to, I might add."

"You dated Harvey Kinkle?" the girl asked incredulously. "Why did you ever give him up?"

Morgan gulped. That hadn't exactly been how it was. In fact, the truth was, Harvey had sort of ended things with her. But Morgan couldn't let this stranger know that. "It seemed like a good idea at the time," she replied cagily.

"Well, I guess that means he's free for the rest of us," the curly locked Harvey admirer said as she moved closer to her favorite Cattitude Dude.

Sabrina looked over at her roommate. Morgan was obviously in shock. For the first time someone was more popular than she was. And that someone was Harvey Kinkle. Obviously, from Morgan's point of view, the whole world was out of kilter.

"Don't worry, Morgan," Sabrina told her. "You can always say that you once dated a TV celebrity. That's got to count for something. Maybe the tabloids will pay you for your story."

Sabrina's sarcasm was lost on Morgan. "Gee, you really think so?" she asked.

Chapter 7

☆

☆

Sabrina bent down and peeked under her bed. Here it was Halloween night, and she was running late. If she didn't find the pair of black panty hose she needed for her Halloween costume, she'd never make it to the party on time. And Sabrina wanted to savor every moment of her favorite holiday.

"Where are they?" Sabrina moaned as she peered among the dust bunnies. She was pretty sure she'd thrown black panty hose under there a couple of weeks ago. But tonight there were no panty hose in sight. Instead, all Sabrina could see was a giant sea of purple boxes.

Kurt had only been Roxie's one-and-only for no more than a day and a half, but he'd already run Sabrina's credit card bill higher than she could've ever imagined. Sabrina had tried to wash one of his shirts so he could wear it again, only to discover that you weren't supposed to wash Kurt doll clothes— not only did they shrink, the colors ran and the threads tore. Never mind how much they cost—Kurt clothes were basically garbage.

Which was why Sabrina was searching through her wardrobe for something to wear. She'd been hoping to rent or buy a spectacular costume, but she was completely out of cash.

"Aha! There you are!" Sabrina exclaimed as she fished the panty hose out from behind an empty box. She held the hose up to the light. Oh good! No runs.

"Hurry up!" Roxie demanded as she put the finishing touches on her makeup and readjusted her wet suit. "Kurt's been waiting out there for hours."

Sabrina sighed. "I'm going as fast as I can," she insisted as she slipped a black leotard on.

Roxie sat down on her bed and smiled at Sabrina. "You know, it's very sweet of you to offer to play chauffeur for Kurt and me," she began slowly. "But it's really not necessary. Kurt can drive me over to the frat house, and you can meet us there." She sounded hopeful.

Sabrina knew what Roxie was saying, and she sympathized with her. But she had no intention of letting her roommate go alone to a frat party with a doll. Sooner or later she'd have to pick up on his lack of verbal skills. Sabrina had to keep the conversation going. Besides, Sabrina didn't know what kind of driver Kurt was. He'd never seen traffic signs or stoplights before. They didn't exist in Betsy world. It was better if Sabrina stayed behind the wheel. "It's okay, Roxie. I love driving," she assured her.

"But it's Kurt's car," Roxie said. "Don't you think he'll want to drive?"

Sabrina shook her head. "Kurt has no idea where the frat house is. And he absolutely hates to ask for directions. You know how guys are. So he and I worked out this plan where I'll drive, and he can snuggle with you in the backseat. "

"He wants to sit in the backseat with me?" Roxie said.

Sabrina nodded. "That way he doesn't have to keep his eyes on the road—he can keep them on you."

That seemed to placate Roxie. She smiled in the mirror and fixed her hair.

Sabrina took a black eyebrow pencil and penciled in some thin whiskers under her nose. Then she pinned on a tail and slipped on a pair of velvety ears.

"Ta-da!" she said, spinning around. "What do you think?" she asked Roxie.

Before the surfer girl could answer, a very frustrated Juliet burst into the room. "Can I borrow a . . . ," Morgan began. Then she caught a glimpse of Sabrina. "Oh no. Not you, too," she moaned.

"Not me too what?" Sabrina asked.

"You're not into that Cattitude thing, too, are you?" she replied, staring at Sabrina's black cat costume.

"I think Sabrina looks cute," Roxie said.

"Thank you," Sabrina replied.

"I'm sick of all things cat," Morgan continued. "That's all anybody around this and every other school is talking about. In fact, the only person around here I can talk to is Kurt. At least he never goes on and on about letting someone else clean up the mess in your litter box. Kurt's the most interesting guy in Boston."

Sabrina choked back a giggle. If Morgan only knew.

"He's pretty amazing," Roxie said quickly. "And he's mine. Don't forget that, Morgan."

"Well, you should be grateful for him. He's probably the only guy on campus who doesn't have sardine breath," Morgan told her. "I swear, this afternoon Harvey ordered sardines and a glass of milk at the cafeteria. He told everyone it was a deli- cacy . . . and they believed him!" Morgan shud- dered. "Sardines! After all I taught that boy about fine dining."

Sabrina to Roxie. "Okay, after you. Your car is waiting."

"Ooh, are you driving over in that purple convert- ible?" Morgan asked hopefully. "It's so kitsch. Really retro. Mind if I hitch a ride with you guys?"

"Some date. Just the four of us," Roxie moaned.

"Don't be so selfish," Morgan scolded her. "It's a big car; we can all fit."

Roxie shrugged. "Sure, why not? Hey, you can even sit up front."

Morgan's face brightened. "I can?" she said incredulously. Morgan thought Kurt was driving. She couldn't understand why Roxie would let her sit next to that sexy hunk. But she wasn't going to question it. Morgan never looked a gift horse in the mouth. She loved gifts too much.

The girls all put jackets on over their costumes for the ride over. It was, after all, fall in Massachu- setts. But Kurt was perfectly content to ride over to the frat house in his bathing suit, tank top, and flip-flops. (He would have to be content. Sabrina hadn't bought him a jacket yet.)

"Aren't you going to be cold?" Morgan asked as they headed toward the car.

"Let's go to the beach!" Kurt replied.

"Um, Kurt has taken some acting classes," Sabrina interjected quickly. "I think he's trying to stay in character. You know, Method acting."

Morgan smiled at him. "You'd be a great actor. You have movie star eyes."

Roxie's face turned red and her eyes bugged.

"What's with you?" Morgan asked her. "You look awful."

"Let it go," Sabrina whispered in Roxie's ear. "He's true blue, remember? He doesn't even know any other girl exists."

Roxie watched as Morgan continued flirting with Kurt. "I hope you're right," she told Sabrina.

"Remember, you said I could sit up front," Morgan said as she hopped into the front passenger seat. Her face fell as Sabrina sat down behind the wheel. "But I thought . . . ," she began. "Why isn't Kurt driving?"

Sabrina smiled. "He'd rather focus his attention on his date."

"That would be me," Roxie reminded her.

"Okay, everyone buckle up." Sabrina turned the hard plastic key in the ignition and put her foot to the purple gas peddle.

"Whoa!" Roxie shouted from the backseat as the car sped down the street. Her body was thrown against the soft furry purple backseat.

"Oops, sorry," Sabrina said as she eased up on the gas. "I'm not used to Kurt's car."

"Don't slow down, I like it!" Roxie shouted over the wind that was blowing around the roofless car.

It wasn't far to the Sigma Kappa Delta house. Before anyone knew it, Sabrina had pulled up front. As Morgan stepped out of the convertible, a group of costumed partiers turned and pointed in her direction.

Morgan smiled benevolently at the crowd. She was used to being noticed. She was not, however, used to being laughed at.

"Check out Morgan," a tall, sinewy guy in a lion costume shouted out.

"Whoa, what happened to you?" A short, chubby fraternity brother in an orange-and-black Garfield costume laughed.

Morgan tried to looked behind her. "Is my dress stuck in my panty hose?" she whispered to Sabrina.

Sabrina shook her head and held back a laugh of her own.

Morgan felt her cheek. "My false eyelashes didn't fall?"

Again, Sabrina shook her head. She clamped her lips tight. It was getting harder and harder to choke the laughter back.

"I love your hair," Kurt blurted out suddenly.

"Oh, you say the nicest things," Morgan replied flirtatiously.

"Yeah, great hair!" the kid in the lion costume remarked—just before he doubled over with laughter.

That did it. The giggling was too contagious. Sabrina started to chuckle. Before long, Roxie was hysterical as well.

"Uh, Morgan," Roxie said, pointing to her own head.

Morgan bent down and peered in the sideview mirror. "Aaaaah!!!!" she screamed out in horror.

Riding in the convertible might have seemed like a good idea at the time, but now she realized what a mistake it had been. Morgan had carefully teased, and brushed, moussed, and gelled every strand of her hair before leaving the house. She'd looked perfect—as elegant as any Juliet ever had. But driving in a car without a roof had been a disaster. Thanks to the wind, Morgan now looked more like the Bride of Frankenstein than the bride of Romeo.

Morgan stared at Kurt. "'I love your hair,'" she repeated in a voice that mimicked his slightly mechanical tone. "Real funny."

"I thought it was," Roxie said, taking Kurt's hand in her own.

"Relax, Morgan, we all have messed-up hair," Sabrina said. "That's part of the convertible experience."

"So what, we're all a mess." Roxie looked up at her handsome escort. "Except you, Kurt. Your hair hasn't moved an inch."

Sabrina gulped. Synthetic hair didn't movie. "Yeah Kurt, you look great," she said quickly. "You'll have to tell us what kind of gel you use. Now let's get inside and start dancing."

"You go ahead. I'm going to go around the corner and fix my hair. I'd rather not make my entrance with you guys anyway."

"Okay, we'll see ya inside," Sabrina said.

"Let's party!" Kurt exclaimed as they walked in the door.

Roxie snuggled up close to Kurt. "That's my boy," she said happily.

Chapter 8

☆

"**H**ey, watch it," a fraternity brother in a spotted leopard costume hissed at Sabrina as she tried to push her way through the crowd. "You'll have to wait your turn to get near Harvey."

Sabrina looked at him strangely. Who said she was looking for Harvey? "I just wanted to get to the dance floor," she told the leopard.

"Oh no! You're not dancing with Harvey before I do," a girl in a black cat costume told Sabrina. "I've been waiting all night to dance with the Cattitude Dude."

Sabrina frowned—and not just because this girl was telling her she'd have to wait for her chance to be near Harvey. She was more upset about how many girls were dressed as black cats. Sabrina usually wore a more original costume on Halloween. Something that really stood out in a crowd. But, of

76

course, that was before the arrival of Kurt.

And speaking of Kurt, he and Roxie were standing next to each other on the dance floor. They weren't moving. Kurt was obviously saying something. But the music was so loud, Roxie couldn't hear him. Which was just as well.

"Sabrina, there you are!" a familiar voice called out from the center of the crowd. "I was wondering when you were going to show."

"Hi, Harvey," Sabrina shouted back.

"Make room for the man," a football player dressed as a tiger proclaimed as Harvey made his way toward Sabrina. "The Cattitude Dude is on the prowl."

Sabrina was aware of the jealous stares she got from the girls in the crowd, but she didn't acknowledge them. Instead, she burst out laughing when Harvey came into view. Sabrina thought for sure he'd be dressed as a cat. But he wasn't. He was covered in straw, and wearing overalls. "What are you supposed to be?" Sabrina asked him.

"The Scarecrow from *The Wizard of Oz.*"

"What happened to the whole Cattitude thing? Shouldn't you be a lion or a tiger, or at the very least a calico?"

Harvey frowned. "Cattitude is a state of mind, not

a Halloween costume," he corrected her. "I always wanted to be the Scarecrow for Halloween. So, that's who I am. I do what I want, when I want. It's what makes me, me."

"It's what makes you irresistible," a girl dressed as an elegant Siamese cat interrupted, slipping her arm around Harvey's waist. "I thought you promised me a dance, Harvey."

Before Harvey could reply, Morgan's acid-toned voice rang out. "Well, look at you," she said as she approached. "The Scarecrow. It fits. If you only had a brain, you'd be dressed as my Romeo rather than some ridiculous straw man."

"What are you supposed to be?" the Siamese cat asked Morgan.

"Juliet, of course. I'm elegant, and I'm royalty."

"Big deal," the girl replied. "In ancient Egypt, royalty worshiped cats. They understood the importance of Cattitude—isn't that true, Harvey?"

Harvey smiled and moved a stick of straw that had almost found its way up his nose. "Exactly true," he agreed.

"You want attitude, I'll give you attitude," Morgan said.

"Not attitude, Morgan—Cattitude," Harvey corrected

her. "There's nothing mean in what we believe. It's simply self-preservation." He moved his hands in front of his face in a catlike motion.

It was very dark in the room, but Sabrina was pretty sure she saw Harvey lick his fingers for just a second. She gulped. He looked just like Salem when he did that—if Salem were dressed as the Scarecrow from *The Wizard of Oz,* anyway.

"Oh Harvey, you're so smart," the Siamese cat girl purred. "Listen. They're playing our song."

As Harvey ran off to dance, Sabrina scanned the room for Roxie and Kurt. She wanted Roxie to have a good time . . . and not discover that her date was an oversize plastic doll. "Excuse me," Sabrina said, moving past Morgan.

"Whatever," Morgan said, her voice distant and aloof. She was staring at Harvey, who was now surrounded by several girls all dressed in different breeds of cat costumes. What a switch. Harvey was the center of attention, and no one seemed to notice Morgan was even at the party. It wasn't Harvey who had been knocked from the popularity radar screen. It was Morgan.

"Hi, guys!" Sabrina shouted over the music as she reached Roxie and Kurt.

"Hi, Sabrina," Roxie said. "Bye, Sabrina."

Sabrina wasn't taking the hint. She was afraid to leave Roxie and Kurt for too long. There was no predicting what he might say.

"Betsy is the coolest," Kurt said.

Sabrina gulped. Like that, for instance.

Luckily, Roxie hadn't caught what Kurt had said. "What?"

"Tennis anyone?"

Roxie shook her head. "Can't hear you," she said as she began to sway slightly to the beat.

As the music came to a mellower section, Kurt looked at Roxie. "Do you want to dance?"

"I'd love to," Roxie said. She took Kurt by the hand and dragged him to the center of the dance floor. Obviously, she wanted everyone to see her hot new man.

Sabrina gulped. She had a feeling Roxie would have been better off in a dark, quiet corner somewhere. She'd never seen a dancing Kurt doll before. She wasn't sure if the joints in his arms and legs were made to bend that way.

Sabrina was right. His dance moves weren't exactly slick. In fact, they were stiff and unbending—almost robotic.

Which seemed to please Roxie a lot. "Look at

him," she shouted toward Sabrina. "He's doing the robot." She turned to Kurt. "You are so retro!" she exclaimed as she, too, began to move in a stiff, robotic motion.

At first the other people on the dance floor stared at Kurt and Roxie in disbelief. There were a few giggles, and some stares. Sabrina frowned. Roxie was becoming a laughingstock. This wasn't what she had in mind at all.

"Oh cool," Harvey shouted. "Look at that Cattitude."

"What are you talking about?" asked a member of the swim team, who was dressed as Winnie the Pooh's pal, Tigger. "They look ridiculous."

Harvey nodded. "They do. But they don't care how the look. They're dancing the way they want to. We can all accept it or not. They don't care."

"You're right," Tigger said.

"What a genius," the Siamese kitten purred.

"Look at me," a tall basketball player in a stray cat costume announced. "I'm doing the robot too."

Before long, everyone was dancing like Kurt. Sabrina looked over at Harvey and smiled.

"Thanks for saving Roxie," she told Harvey as she made her way across the dance floor.

Harvey shrugged. "I just said what I thought."

"But you made everyone agree with you."

"Of course," Harvey replied confidently. "You can get mortals to agree with anything—as long as you say it with enough conviction."

"Mortals?" Sabrina said.

Harvey nodded. "Mere mortals, anyway."

"You sound like Salem," Sabrina said.

"Thanks for the compliment," Harvey answered.

Sabrina sighed. She hadn't necessarily meant it as a compliment.

"How come you haven't purchased a Cattitude tape yet, Sabrina?" Harvey asked. "I'm sure Salem would give you a discount. After all, you're family."

Sabrina laughed. Harvey obviously didn't know Salem as well as he thought. Salem wouldn't even give his own mother a discount.

"I've witnessed Cattitude up close for a long time," Sabrina assured Harvey. "I don't think I need a tape."

"You're so lucky, Sabrina," Harvey told her.

"Why?"

"Because you've lived with Salem."

"'Lucky''s not exactly the first word that comes to mind, Harv."

"No, I'm serious," Harvey insisted. "He's a genius. I'm sure you've learned a lot from him."

82

Sabrina grimaced. All she'd ever learned from Salem was how to get in trouble. Every time she'd taken advice from her cat she'd wound up in the middle of a messed up spell and endless aggravation. But she didn't bother explaining that to Harvey. He'd never believe her. He'd have to learn that lesson for himself.

As she danced with Harvey, Sabrina glanced over at Kurt and Roxie. They were having a great time. Or at least Roxie was. Kurt had the same expression on his face that he always did: a sort of half smile and a mindless stare.

As the last notes of the song blared from the speakers, Kurt smiled at Roxie. "Want to share a soda?" he asked.

Roxie nodded. "Sounds good."

Kurt turned and headed off toward the bar. Almost instantly, a crowd of flirtatious female kittens followed after him.

"Wow, are you cute," said a cheerleader dressed as a black kitten.

"And feel those muscles," a tall, thin girl in a cheetah suit added as she squeezed Kurt's considerable bicep.

A girl with a very curvy figure wearing a low-cut, fluffy white kitten costume ran her hand seductively across Kurt's face. "Oooh, what smooth skin," she said. "It's like you never have to shave. And you don't have a pimple anywhere. What's your secret?"

"Purple is my favorite color," Kurt replied.

"Mine too," a small blonde in a leopard costume interjected. "Some people say my eyes are so blue, they're almost purple."

As the girls flirted with Kurt, Sabrina caught a glimpse of Roxie. Her big brown eyes looked sad—but they weren't tearing up. Roxie didn't cry. She got even. So while her eyes might have been sad, her face was burning mad. A little vein had popped up in her neck. Sabrina knew that vein well. It was like a warning sign. Steer clear!

Not good at all.

"Excuse me, Harvey," Sabrina said quickly. "I think Roxie might need me." She quickly raced across the room. "Hey Rox, havin' a good time?" she asked with hope as she pulled up beside her.

"Look at him," Roxie told Sabrina. "He's such a flirt. I told you this would happen. True blue—yeah, right."

"Kurt doesn't look like he's flirting with those girls. They're flirting with him," Sabrina corrected her.

"And the difference would be?"

"It's a big difference," Sabrina assured her. "Think

about it. Kurt only has eyes for you, trust me. He's not interested in those girls."

"I don't see him blowing them off," Roxie argued.

"That wouldn't be polite," Sabrina replied. "He'll be back."

"Let's hope," Roxie said. But she didn't sound at all hopeful.

"Trust me," Sabrina said.

Roxie sighed. "Okay. But if he does come back, do you think you could disappear for a while? I mean, no offense Sabrina, but frankly, three's becoming a major crowd."

"But I . . . um . . . er . . . ," Sabrina stammered nervously. There was no rational excuse she could give for her tagalong behavior. At least no excuse Roxie would ever believe. Sabrina didn't know what to say.

But Kurt did. "Let's party!" he exclaimed as he came back to where the two girls were standing. He handed Roxie a cold soda.

Roxie practically glowed as she took the plastic cup from Kurt's hand.

"Told ya so," Sabrina whispered in her ear.

"Get lost," Roxie whispered back.

But Sabrina had no intention of leaving Roxie alone with Kurt.

"Fish sticks and milk in the poolroom!" one of the frat brothers suddenly shouted out. "First come, first serve!"

Sabrina blanched. Fish sticks and milk at a frat party? Whatever happened to beer and pretzels?

Apparently, Sabrina was in the minority when it came to her menu preferences. Fish and milk was the perfect party treat for the Cattitude crowd.

Almost instantly, the crowd of partiers headed off the dance floor in a mad rush for the poolroom. Everyone wanted their fish and milk. No one wanted to be left out.

Sabrina was standing in the crowd's path. She had only two choices: Move with them, or risk being trampled by them. Suddenly she felt herself being carried off with the crowd. "Roxie, help!" she shouted out. But Roxie couldn't hear Sabrina.

"Want to go for a drive?" Roxie asked Kurt.

"Tennis anyone?" he answered.

Roxie shook her head. "I thought we could drive somewhere where we could be alone and talk."

"I'll pick you up in my car," Kurt answered her.

Roxie laughed. "Purple is my favorite color," she assured him.

Chapter 9

"**W**ahoo!" Roxie yelled out into the crisp October night. "Put your pedal to the metal!"

Kurt was speeding down Main Street, blowing through red lights and forcing the other cars on the road to move over. Having never driven on a real street, Kurt had no idea how fast to go, or what to do when he saw other cars on the road. And he'd never seen an actual red light—everything in the world of Betsy dolls was purple, after all.

"You're a wild man!" Roxie laughed. "I'll bet this is a side of you Sabrina has never seen."

"Let's party," Kurt said.

Before Roxie could answer, the sound of police sirens came screaming from behind. Roxie could see the red lights flashing in the sideview mirror. "You'd better pull over," she told him.

But Kurt didn't know how to pull over. He didn't even know how to stop the car. Dolls never really did their own driving. Little girls did that for them. Their giant human hands moved the car across the floor. The dolls went along for the ride.

"Kurt, stop," Roxie urged. Speeding through town had been fun, but the sight of those lights scared her.

"Let's go to the beach," Kurt said.

"You're going to get a ticket," Roxie told him.

But Kurt didn't even know what tickets were. They didn't exist in the world of Betsy and Kurt. So Kurt kept driving, past the mall, the mini-mart, and the school yard. In fact, he and Roxie were practically halfway to Vermont before the car came to a sudden stop.

Roxie looked over at the dashboard. "We're out of gas," she told Kurt.

"Betsy is the coolest," Kurt responded.

Now Roxie was mad. It was one thing to outrun a cop. It was another thing entirely to talk about some other girl. "Excuse me?" she demanded, the vein in her neck beginning to throb.

Before Kurt could say anything else, a police-woman shined a flashlight in his eyes. Can I have your license, please?" she asked.

Kurt gave her a blank stare.

"License?" the police officer asked again.

Kurt still didn't move.

"Look, you'd better do as I say, young man. You're in a lot of trouble. Do you have any idea how fast you were going? Or how many red lights you went through? You have enough moving violations from this one joy ride to get your license revoked. Now driver's license, please."

Kurt seemed confused.

"I, um, maybe it's in the glove compartment," Roxie told her.

"Okay, open it slowly. And don't try anything funny," the police officer ordered.

Roxie opened the glove compartment and pulled out a rectangle-shape piece of paper. "Here you go," she said.

The police officer took the paper from Roxie and held it under the light. "What is this, some sort of joke?" the police officer demanded. "I don't feel very much like laughing right now, you two."

Roxie looked at her. "Joke?" she said. "Why would I joke?"

The police officer held the paper so Roxie could

see better. Instead of a driver's license, the sheet of paper was filled with pictures of purple boats, bikes, and motor homes, all just the right size for eleven-and-a-half-inch Betsy and Kurt dolls.

"All right, out of the car," the police officer ordered. She turned her body so Kurt could see the gun in her holster. This officer clearly meant business.

But Kurt had never seen a gun. He had no idea what it was. He wasn't at all upset by the sight of the weapon. "Let's go for pizza," he said.

Sabrina was standing outside the frat house when her cell phone rang. She reached into her jacket pocket and pulled out the phone. "Hello?"

"Sabrina, am I glad I got you," Roxie said.

"Where are you? I've been looking all over."

"Well, it's a long story," Roxie began. "Kurt and I took a drive, and we ran out of gas, and now . . ."

"Never mind all that, where are you?" Sabrina demanded.

"In jail."

At first, Sabrina was silent in disbelief. "Roxie, I think we have a bad connection," she said finally. "It sounded like you said you were in jail."

"I did."

"Why?" Sabrina demanded.

"Because that's where we are."

Sabrina sighed. "No. Not why did you say that. Why are you in jail?"

"I told you, we had a little car trouble. This policewoman came. Kurt was carrying some doll advertisement and he asked her to go for pizza." Roxie paused for a moment. "Sabrina, do you know anyone named Betsy?"

"What does Betsy have to do with you being in jail?"

"Nothing," Roxie admitted. "It's just that Kurt mentioned her before we got arrested."

"She's no one. An old girlfriend," Sabrina replied.

"Oh, thank goodness." Roxie gave a sigh of relief.

So did Sabrina. In all the excitement of being in jail, Roxie obviously wasn't making the connection between Kurt and Betsy the dolls, and Kurt the living doll.

Still, it did strike Sabrina as more than a little bizarre that Roxie cared more about Kurt's past love life than the fact she was in jail.

"I'll be right there," Sabrina told Roxie.

* * *

"Oh Sabrina, you wouldn't believe how amazing Kurt was. There we were, flying through the streets like renegades. Nothing could stop us," Roxie could barely contain herself when she and Sabrina met up at the police station. She was talking a mile a minute and practically glowing.

Sabrina had seen Roxie like this before. She'd had the same look on her face when she was arrested after last month's antinuclear arms rally, and when she was arrested for picketing a fur coat store with some other members of PETA. Getting arrested really agreed with Roxie.

"Cars ran out of the way to let us through," Roxie continued. "And then, when the police stopped us, Kurt wasn't afraid. He didn't care that she had a gun or a badge. He just turned to her and said, 'Do you want to go for pizza?' I'm telling you, it was inspiring."

"You like that he speeds when he drives and that he ignores a policewoman's orders?" Sabrina asked her in disbelief.

"A lack of respect for authority is something I really like in a person, Sabrina. It was so thrilling. I felt like we were Bonnie and Clyde."

"Nice role models, Roxie," Sabrina said.

Roxie made a face. "You know what I mean. It was all so on the edge. I'm telling you, Sabrina, your old friend Kurt is a real bad boy!"

Just then a policeman came through the door with Bad Boy Kurt beside him. "Here's the other one," he told Sabrina. He handed her a ticket. "You can pay the fine at the door."

Sabrina opened her bag and fished out her wallet. Roxie reached out a hand to stop her. "Don't you pay a cent, Sabrina," Roxie told her.

"I thought you said you didn't have any money with you."

"I don't," Roxie agreed. "But we shouldn't have to pay any fine. It says on that ticket that Kurt refused to show the officer his license. He didn't refuse."

"He didn't?" Sabrina asked.

Roxie shook her head. "He doesn't have a license. That's different."

"And what about this resisting arrest thing?"

"He didn't resist arrest. He just asked the police officer to come with us for pizza."

"It says on this ticket you were going 110 miles an hour down Main Street!" Sabrina exclaimed. "Don't you think you guys deserved to be pulled over?"

Roxie shrugged.

"Forget it, Roxie," Sabrina told her. "I'll pay the ticket."

"But we should go to court. Fight the system." Roxie took Kurt by the arm and smiled up at him.

"Let's party!" Kurt added.

"See?" Roxie said proudly.

There was no way Sabrina was letting Kurt take one step near a courtroom. Who knew what he might say to a judge! "Forget it. We're paying the fine," Sabrina insisted.

"But Sabrina, it's two hundred fifty dollars!" Roxie told her.

Sabrina let out a little moan. That was a lot of money.

"Okay, let's go jailbirds," Sabrina said as she ripped the check from her checkbook and tucked her wallet away. She headed for the door of the police station. Roxie and Kurt followed close behind.

"What time is it?" Roxie asked as the trio stepped out into the cool night air.

Sabrina checked her watch. "Twelve fifty-five," she replied with a frown. Halloween was over, and all she had to show for it was an empty wallet. "What a lousy holiday."

"I thought it was great," Roxie said, smiling up at Kurt.

Sabrina shook her head. Roxie had spent Halloween listening to bad music (just how many times can one fraternity DJ play "Stray Cat Strut," anyway?), drinking flat soda, and getting arrested. Not exactly a normal person's definition of a great night. Further proof that Roxie was not a normal person.

Sabrina thought back on the Halloweens she'd spent with her aunts. Those had been happy times . . . well, sort of. There was that family dinner when her bratty cousin Amanda had locked her in a jar for a while, but for the most part, Halloween brought back warm, cozy memories. Until now, that is. "Better luck next year," Sabrina muttered quietly to herself.

"What?" Roxie asked her.

"Never mind. Let's just go home."

Roxie brightened. "Speaking of homes . . . Kurt, I'd love to see your house. I'll bet it's amazing!"

"I'll pick you up in my car!" Kurt replied enthusiastically.

"Oh great! We can go tomorrow after my science lab," Roxie agreed.

Sabrina let out a small moan. This was not good. It meant she was going to have to buy a home for

Kurt. And somehow she had a feeling there wasn't any low-rent college housing in the Betsy and Kurt collection.

"I thought Kurt's car was towed," Sabrina reminded Roxie. "He can't drive you anywhere." There was no way she was paying to get the purple convertible released. If Roxie wanted to ride around in style, she could go down to the city garage and pay the bill.

"Oh, that's okay. I can walk," Roxie said. "Kurt lives right near your aunts—right, Sabrina?"

"Uh yeah, right next door," Sabrina answered quietly. She wondered how her aunts would feel when a purple Kurt and Betsy town house sprang up in their backyard.

"That's not far at all. I can get there around four thirty, okay Kurt?"

Kurt nodded. Then he looked out at the street. "Let's go to the beach," he said.

Sabrina shook her head. "Not tonight, kids. It's late. We have to go home."

"Who are you, my mother?" Roxie asked.

Sabrina shook her head. "No, I'm the person who just paid a two hundred fifty dollar ticket for Roxie and Kurt's big adventure. And Rox, you have class tomorrow!"

Roxie couldn't argue with that. "Okay, you win," she said. "We'll go home. At least you and I can spend tomorrow afternoon at your house, Kurt. We can listen to music and chill out."

Sabrina glanced over at Roxie's happy face. She seemed really crazy about Kurt. Sabrina was happy for her best friend. It was great that Roxie had found someone she liked. Unfortunately, Sabrina knew it couldn't last. Roxie and Kurt were from two different worlds. Hers was the real world, and his was . . . well . . . manufactured. Eventually Roxie would discover that they had nothing common.

Besides, Sabrina wasn't sure just how much longer she could afford to keep bankrolling Roxie's romance.

Chapter 10

☆

"**A**nybody home?" Sabrina shouted out as she lugged four heavy bags of toys up the stairs of Zelda and Hilda's two-story house. But it was already 11:00 in the morning. Hilda and Zelda were long gone and had never realized that Kurt had spent the night in Sabrina's old room.

But Kurt was home. "Purple is my favorite color," he called back down to her. He didn't seem at all tired after his Halloween crime spree. Dolls, after all, didn't require any sleep.

But college students did. Sabrina was exhausted.

"Do you want to dance?"

Sabrina sighed. Kurt's ten exciting phrases were getting old. "Stay right there," she told Kurt. "I'll be right up."

It took Sabrina a little longer than usual to get up

the stairs. It was hard to walk under the weight of a Betsy and Kurt town house, four full rooms' worth of Betsy and Kurt furniture, and a real working Betsy and Kurt CD player (just in case Kurt asked Roxie to dance . . . again). When she finally reached her old room, she collapsed onto the bed, spilling the packages all over the mattress. "I've got to get to the gym more often," she huffed.

"Tennis anyone?" Kurt asked.

Sabrina rolled her eyes. "Very funny." She pointed to the toy store bags beside her. "You should be nice to me. Look what I got you." She reached into the bag and pulled out a box of living room furniture.

Kurt held the box in his hand and studied the picture on the front: It showed him sitting on the couch, with his charming half smile. His face was tilted down just a bit so it looked as though he was looking lovingly at the beautiful Betsy doll beside him.

"Betsy is the coolest!" Kurt said as he quickly began opening all the bags. The big guy looked like a kid at Christmas (or a witch at Halloween!) as he examined each and every purchase. He was obviously happy to see all his things around him. He seemed more comfortable somehow, more relaxed.

"Hey, what's all that?" Harvey shouted out. He leaped down from his spot atop Sabrina's window and landed perfectly on all fours.

"Aaah!" Sabrina cried out with surprise. "Harvey, where did you come from?"

"I've been here since early this morning," Harvey told her. "I'm waiting for Salem. We're supposed to have a meeting."

"Why didn't you say something when I asked if anyone was here? You were so quiet, I had no idea."

Harvey smiled and smoothed the whiskerlike mustache beneath his nose. "I know. I've been working on that. I can sit completely still . . . waiting."

"Waiting for what?" Sabrina asked.

"I don't know," Harvey admitted. "That's one of the things I had to talk to Salem about. All I know is I'm supposed to learn to sit still, and gain patience. I have to learn when to pounce. Speaking of which, did you like my landing? I think I only bruised one knee this time."

"It was great," Sabrina said. "Honestly."

"Betsy is the coolest," Kurt blurted out as he stared at the box that held the CD player.

"You know, that guy's really weird," Harvey said suddenly. "What's with the Betsy doll obsession?"

"Mine or his?" Sabrina asked.

"Either. Both."

"Long story," Sabrina said. "You don't want to know."

"Probably not," Harvey agreed. He'd learned long ago not to ask Sabrina too many personal questions. He quickly changed the subject. "Isn't he the guy Roxie was with at the party last night?"

Sabrina nodded.

"Why do I think there's more to that guy than meets the eye?" Harvey asked Sabrina.

"Actually, there's probably less to him than meets the eye," Sabrina replied. "In fact, he's not a real guy exactly. He's more of a—"

"Don't tell me," Harvey said. "I have a feeling this is one of those witch stories that I'm better off not knowing anything about. In fact, I'm going to go now. Just tell Salem I was here." Harvey glanced in the mirror. "Oh no!" he exclaimed.

"What?" Sabrina asked him.

"I have a hair out of place!" Harvey exclaimed. He licked his fingers and used the spit to smooth out his hair. "Ah, that's better. Clean and neat. That's the Cattitude way!" Then he turned and quietly padded his way downstairs.

Sabrina was relieved to hear the front door close as Harvey left. She didn't really want to have to explain Kurt's origins to him. Oh sure, Harvey would understand the witchcraft part of it. And he could definitely relate to the problems Sabrina's spell was causing. After all, he'd been swept up in a few bad spells before himself.

But chances are, Harvey would tell Sabrina something she already knew deep down: Bringing Kurt into Roxie's life had been a big mistake. Roxie was only going to get hurt. Sure, Roxie would have a good time tonight in Kurt's state-of-the-art town house. And maybe they'd share a few more romantic sodas and a game of tennis together. But sooner or later, Sabrina was going to have to zap Kurt back to his normal size and out of Roxie's life. And the longer this relationship went on, the more upset Roxie would be when it had to end.

Sabrina sighed. Maybe she should just end this thing right now. Just zap Kurt down to his original eleven-and-a-half inches. She could always come up with something to tell Roxie that would make things less painful. Like a story about Kurt joining the Peace Corps and going off to help poor people in some village in Southeast Asia where there were no

phones or computers. Roxie would like that. At least Kurt would be doing something noble.

No doubt about it, Sabrina had to end this thing now—before Roxie got in too deep . . . and while she could still return the town house, the four rooms of furniture, and the CD player.

Sabrina quickly turned and faced Kurt. Before he even knew what was happening, Sabrina waved her magic finger.

"It's been fun, and quite romantic.
But Roxie needs a break, and I'm going frantic.
Kurt's sure handsome at six foot three,
but it's time to return to the size he should be."

Sabrina stood back and waited for the magical flash of light that usually followed her spells. But nothing happened. Kurt was still sitting on the bed surrounded by boxes of Betsy toys.

Oh no! Was there something wrong with her finger? Was her magic going bad?

Sabrina quickly looked down at her jeans. They were plain blue and a little worn. She wiggled her finger. There was a flash of light, and then, suddenly, Sabrina's classic jeans were decorated with laces along the sides and rhinestones on the belt loops.

No, there was nothing wrong with her magic. Or her fashion sense, for that matter. So why couldn't she zap Kurt back to doll size?

Maybe a different spell would work. Sabrina pointed at Kurt and wiggled her finger once again. *"This guy isn't a real boy. It's time to turn back to a toy."*

Nothing happened.

"Let's go for a pizza," Kurt suggested.

"Aaargh!" Sabrina moaned.

Just then the front door opened and closed. One of Sabrina's aunts had come home. Surely they'd be able to help her . . . after they scolded her. Oh well. She had no other choice. Sabrina turned and went down the stairs.

"Sabrina, what a nice surprise!" her aunt Zelda greeted her.

"Aunt Zelda, I need your help," Sabrina cried.

"Nice to see you, too." Zelda frowned. "Can't you at least say hello before you ask for my help?"

"Hello. Now can you help me?"

Zelda laughed. "Of course. But I only have a few minutes. I'm due at a conference in half an hour. I just stopped home to get my notes."

Sabrina headed up the stairs. "It won't take that long.

I just need you to help me figure out the right spell."

"The right spell for what?" Zelda asked as she followed Sabrina into her room.

"For that," Sabrina said, pointing to Kurt.

Zelda's eyes opened wide. "Who is that man? And what is he doing sitting on your bed, in girls' pajamas?"

"It's not what you think, Aunt Zelda," Sabrina assured her. "He's actually Roxie's boyfriend," Sabrina continued. "Well, not boyfriend exactly. Not even a boy, exactly."

"He looks like one to me."

"He's . . ." Sabrina took a deep breath and then just said it. "He's a fashion doll. I just kind of blew him up and brought him to life."

"Why would you do that?" Zelda asked.

"So Roxie would have a date for the party who wasn't an octopus or a snake," Sabrina explained.

Zelda shook her head. "I'm not even going to ask you to translate that into English." She gave Sabrina a disappointed look. "You should never get involved with the love lives of mortals. It's always a disaster."

"Now you tell me." Sabrina sighed.

Zelda looked at her watch. "I don't have much time. Tell me what you need to do."

"I want to zap him back to his old size. But I can't seem to get the spell right. Do you know what I need to chant?"

"Well, that would depend on what spell you used to bring him to life. What exactly did you say?" Zelda asked.

Sabrina thought back to that day in the mall. What was it she'd said? Oh yeah.

"Roxie needs a hottie who'll treat her right.
A guy who'll be there day and night.
Someone to treat her as she deserves.
And really won't get on her nerves.
Kurt's got his own car, and a tux that's black.
He's a crush for Roxie who crushes back!
So hurry up and don't ask why.
Make this Kurt a real live guy."

Zelda frowned. "Well, there's your problem," she stated simply.

"What?"

"You can't turn him back."

Sabrina's eyes nearly popped out of her head. "What do you mean I can't turn him back?"

"You made it clear in your spell that Roxie and

Kurt would have crushes on each other. You can't break that spell until both parties get over their crushes," Zelda explained.

"Oh great!" Sabrina moaned. "Roxie's never going to get over him."

"I love your hair," Kurt interrupted.

Zelda brightened. "Why, thank you. I just had a little trim." She turned to Sabrina. "You do have a problem, Sabrina. I can see why Roxie is so crazy about him. This Kurt fellow is charming."

"Um, Aunt Zelda, he doesn't really mean what he says," Sabrina told her.

"Oh Sabrina, don't be silly. My hair does look good today. I just got it cut so I could look perfect for this conference. It was so nice of you to notice," she added, smiling at Kurt.

"Want to share a soda?" Kurt asked.

Zelda smiled. "Maybe some other time. I have to hurry now." And with that, she ran for the door.

"Aunt Zelda, wait!" Sabrina shouted, running after her.

"I can't. I'm late already. Good luck."

Sabrina sat down on the stairs and sighed. This was awful. There was only one thing to do. "Come on, Kurt," she said. "We have a house to decorate."

Chapter 11

"Hey, got any sardines in there?"

Sabrina jumped back as a huge, muscular football player leaped down in front of her, demanding sardines from her backpack. She was surprised. Usually, football players didn't just fall from the sky.

Sabrina rubbed her eyes. She figured maybe a whole morning of playing decorate-the-dollhouse with Kurt had her so tired, she was delusional. But when she opened her eyes, the football player was still there. No. This was completely real.

"Hey, I asked you a question," the football player said. "I'm expressing my needs and desires. I need a good tin of sardines. That at least demands an answer." He smiled proudly. "I learned that on my Cattitude tape."

Cattitude. Sabrina was getting really tired of hearing

that word. "No," she told the football player. "I don't have any sardines with me. I don't even like them." She reached into her backpack and pulled out a small white candy. "I have a Tic Tac, though. It's got a little lint on it, but you can wipe it off."

"Never mind," the football player said. "I'll try the fast-food place at the student center. I heard they have a sardines-and-liver special today. Yum!"

Sardines and liver at a fast-food joint? Sabrina felt queasy.

As the football player scampered off, Sabrina heard a strange rustling coming from high atop one of the trees at the edge of the campus.

"Help! I can't get down," a girl's voice cried out.

Sabrina used her hands to shield her eyes from the sun as looked up. There were three cheerleaders perched on the top branches of an old oak.

"Hey, you, the Cattitude Dude's friend," a cheerleader with long red hair called down to Sabrina. "Do you have a cell phone?"

"Yeah," Sabrina called back up.

"Great. Dial 911, would ya?" she asked. "We need the fire department to come and help us get down."

Sabrina was about to ask what the girls were

doing up there in the first place, when she spied a small black cat strut in front of her.

Salem! Every time he crossed her path, there was trouble.

The cat leaped up on her shoulder. "Better make the call, Sabrina," Salem hissed quietly, so only she could hear. "They can't get down."

"None of them? You mean this has happened before?"

"Thirty-seven times today alone," Salem snickered.

"Why would college students climb up in a tree?" she asked Salem suspiciously. "What have you done?"

"Sabrina, I'm insulted," Salem insisted. "What would make you think I had anything to do with this?"

"Just a hunch."

"It's a simple misunderstanding," Salem assured her. "All I did was have Harvey offer some Cattitude advice on our instructional tape. 'See things from a different perspective. Climb to new heights.' Can I help it if these humans took it too literally?" The cat looked up and started laughing. "Stupid people tricks. It's great entertainment. Better than anything on cable."

Salem licked his front paw. "But seriously, Sabrina, Cattitude is really a hit. The profits are just rolling in. By the way, have you ordered your tape yet?"

Sabrina rolled her eyes.

"Don't knock it till you've tried it, sister. Ya know, you haven't had a date in a while. A little Cattitude might be just the ticket to your lack of love life," Salem suggested.

"Forget it, Salem. I'm not buying any tickets or tapes or any of your Cattitude."

"All I'm saying is . . ." Salem shrugged his shoulders and looked incredibly bored. Textbook Cattitude.

"Just how long do you think you can keep selling these tapes before people realize that you're just ripping them off?" Sabrina asked the cat.

"You know what? P. T. Barnum said there's a sucker born every minute. And from the looks of my bank account, we're in the middle of a baby boom."

"Hey, are you going to call the fire department or what?" one of the stranded cheerleaders demanded. "I have to get to my English class."

"Empowered, huh?" Sabrina asked the cat as she dialed the emergency number on her cell phone.

Sabrina knew Salem had gone too far. He just couldn't

seem to control his need to rule the world. He wanted all these people to be under his spell, and since he didn't have any actual powers anymore, this was as close as he was going to get. Unfortunately, from the look of things, it was working. Sabrina just hoped the Witches' Council didn't get word of Salem's scheme. She really didn't feel like having to change Salem's litter box for another hundred years.

As serious as the Cattitude problem was, Sabrina had more pressing issues to deal with right now. She had to intercept Roxie before she headed over to Kurt's town house on her own. Sabrina had finished decorating the house in record time. She'd managed to get the CD player working—although it only seemed to play one CD: a collection of advertisements for Kurt and Betsy. Her only hope was that for a dedicated headbanger like Roxie, love wasn't just blind, it was deaf, too.

The one thing Sabrina hadn't been able to figure out, though, was how to get the kitchen appliances to work. The only thing you could put in the oven was a giant-size plastic steak. Not exactly gourmet. Still, Sabrina figured Roxie and Kurt could order pizza, since that seemed to be the only food he was programmed to enjoy. Unless, of course, soda counted as a food—although Sabrina wasn't quite sure which of the four major groups that would fit into.

Sabrina was pretty certain she had covered all the bases when putting the town house together—although the directions had been in Japanese, and there might be a screw loose somewhere. You never could tell.

That chance that something could go wrong in this house was the reason Sabrina found herself spending the next half hour hiding behind a bush outside of the science building, watching and waiting for Roxie to emerge. When she finally spied her friend, she leaped out from the shrubs and casually strolled in Roxie's direction.

"What a surprise!" Sabrina exclaimed, trying to act as though the meeting was completely by change. "Fancy meeting you here."

"Surprise? I'm always here on Mondays at four o'clock. It's when my science lab ends. You know that." She looked curiously at Sabrina's head. "Why do you have pine needles in your hair?

Sabrina reached up and pulled a few pieces of shrubbery from her long blond locks. "Oh, is this your lab day?" Sabrina asked, pretending to be innocent. "I guess I forgot. So, what're you up to? Want to go to the mall or something?"

Roxie sighed. "I'm going over to Kurt's house."

"You are?" Sabrina asked.

"Let me guess, you forgot all about that, too, right?" Roxie snapped. She didn't sound like she believed it for a minute.

"Exactly," Sabrina said. "But as long as I'm here, I can walk over with you."

"I can find the house by myself, Sabrina," Roxie said. "He's your aunts' next-door neighbor. I know where Hilda and Zelda live. I think I can take it from there."

"Yeah, he's their next-door neighbor," Sabrina agreed. "But do you know which next door?"

Roxie thought about that. "Come to think of it, he didn't give me an address or anything."

"Then it's a lucky thing I bumped into you."

"Yeah, real lucky." Roxie didn't sound as happy about their fortuitous meeting as Sabrina did.

Sabrina and Roxie didn't say anything during the short hike over to Hilda and Zelda's neighborhood. Roxie certainly didn't seem in a communicative mood. In fact, every time she even glanced in Sabrina's direction she would let out a little grunt or groan.

Sabrina knew better than to get all chatty when Roxie was like that. Considering the fact that it was her presence that was making Roxie hostile, it was definitely best to walk in silence.

Finally, it was Roxie who broke the silence. "That's weird," she said, as she stood outside Sabrina's aunts' house.

"What is?"

"I've been here a dozen times, at least, and I've never noticed that big purple town house before."

Sabrina gulped. She hadn't thought of that. "Um . . . well . . . up until a few days ago, it was pretty well camouflaged."

"Camouflaged?"

"Yeah, it sort of blended in with the trees," Sabrina said, thinking as fast as she could.

"Purple trees?"

"Lavender," Sabrina said.

"Lavender trees?" Roxie asked suspiciously.

"Sure. Where did you think lavender bath soap came from?" Sabrina said.

"Soap doesn't come from trees, Sabrina," Roxie told her.

"Of course not. I knew that." Sabrina laughed

nervously. "I just meant that the house was obscured by trees. But Kurt's family had a bunch of them cut down."

"Trees?" Roxie asked. "I don't remember any trees."

"Well, you can forget about them now," Sabrina told her. "They're gone."

Roxie just stood there, staring at the big purple town house. "Still, I think I would have noticed a house being practically in your aunts' backyard."

"Not necessarily. You usually come in through the front yard."

Roxie shook her head. "That's not the point. I mean, look at that house. It's three stories tall. And it's purple. It would have been hard to miss. Are you sure it's always been there?"

Sabrina nodded. "I remember Kurt's house from when I was just a kid. Even before I lived with Zelda and Hilda." Sabrina looked away. That wasn't a total lie . . . she'd had a Betsy and Kurt town house when she was a little girl. It was just smaller . . . a lot smaller.

"Weird," Roxie repeated.

"Are we going to just stand here all day, or are we going inside?" Sabrina asked, in a desperate attempt to change the subject.

"We?" Roxie demanded. "Why is it you're always around on my dates?"

"Oh, is this a date?" Sabrina asked innocently.

"Yeah," Roxie told her.

"Oops. My mistake. Don't worry. I'll just stop by for a minute. Then I'll make myself scarce." She smiled at Roxie. "Besides, how much trouble can you two get into? I mean, Kurt's car's still impounded, right?"

"Very funny," Roxie groaned. "There's nothing I can say to keep you from coming in with me, is there?"

Sabrina shook her head.

"Fine," Roxie huffed. "Just make sure you don't overstay your welcome, okay? This is a very important evening for me."

"You got it," Sabrina assured her.

Roxie reached down to smooth her lavender-and-tan peasant blouse. "Do I look all right?" she asked.

"I love your hair," Sabrina assured her.

Chapter 12

☆

☆

Sabrina reached forward and gently knocked on the door of Kurt's town house. She didn't want to pound too hard. She was liable to knock the plastic door right off of its plastic hinges.

They just didn't make toys the way they used to.

"He'll never hear that," Roxie told her. "Just ring the doorbell."

"No. Don't . . . ," Sabrina began. But it was too late. As soon as Roxie rang the bell, the Betsy and Kurt advertising jingle tune rang out.

"What a strange bell," Roxie said. But she obviously didn't recognize the song.

Kurt opened the door with the same half smile he always had. "Let's go to the beach!" he greeted them.

"No way, buster," Roxie said with a smile. "You're not getting rid of me so fast. I want to see your place.

What's the matter? Didn't you get a chance to clean up for me?" She pushed her way through the door and into the living room. "Wow!" she said. "This place is amazing. And it's so neat. It doesn't even look like anyone really lives here."

"Kurt's been cleaning all day," Sabrina interjected quickly.

"Purple is my favorite color," Kurt added.

Roxie smiled. "You noticed," she said, running her hands along the hem of her lavender-and-tan peasant blouse.

"Let's party!" Kurt exclaimed.

Sabrina plopped down on the couch and smiled at Kurt and Roxie. "Sounds good to me," she said.

"Don't get too comfortable," Roxie said in Sabrina's ear.

"Let's go for pizza!" Kurt suggested.

"Pizza sounds great," Roxie agreed. "But let's call in. We can have a cozy dinner—for two— right here."

Sabrina knew what Roxie meant, but she pretended not to have heard. "I'll call Garlic Joe's," she suggested. "They make the best pizzas."

"Oh, not Garlic Joe's," Roxie said. "I don't want garlic breath tonight."

But Sabrina was already on her cell phone putting

in the order. "Yes, I'll have one large pie," Sabrina said. She looked over at Roxie, who was already snuggling up beside Kurt on the couch. "With anchovies and extra garlic," she added.

Roxie scowled at her.

"Want to share a soda?" Kurt asked.

"And three large sodas," Sabrina added.

"Better make yours to go," Roxie told Sabrina. She turned to Kurt. "This house is amazing," she told him. "You grew up here, right?"

"He sure did," Sabrina interrupted.

"I'm talking to Kurt," Roxie told her. "So," she asked him, "do you live here alone, or are your parents still here with you?"

The brunette held her breath. If there was one thing Roxie hated, it was a momma's boy. And any guy Kurt's age who lived with his mom would qualify.

"Betsy is the coolest!" Kurt announced.

Roxie's face turned red with anger. She looked as though she'd been slapped across the face. "What did you say?"

Sabrina gasped. Poor Roxie. If she thought Kurt was still in love with Betsy, she'd be sure that he was just a two-timing creep. And then she'd never believe in true love . . . ever. As much as Sabrina wanted this relationship to end, she couldn't let it happen this way. Roxie was her best friend. She didn't want her scarred for life.

"Uh, Betsy . . ." Sabrina had to think fast. "His sister. She talked his parents into letting Kurt live here after they moved to Florida. He's really attached to this place."

"But I thought you said his ex-girlfriend's name was Betsy," Roxie asked accusingly.

"It—it is," Sabrina stammered. "And . . . it's his sister. I mean, they're both named Betsy. He didn't date his sister or anything. Some coincidence, huh?"

"Yeah, some coincidence," Roxie skeptically agreed.

"Do you want to dance?" Kurt asked Roxie.

"Sure. Let me pick a CD," Roxie replied.

Sabrina thought of the lone Betsy and Kurt disc sitting in the lavender CD player. Dancing? Not a good idea. "Hey, I know something we can all do," Sabrina announced. "Let's play charades. That's a fun game. It doesn't require any talking. I'll start."

A few minutes later, as Sabrina was busy acting out the movie title, *To Kill a Mockingbird*, the Betsy and Kurt advertising jingle doorbell rang in the front hall.

"All right. The pizza's here!" Roxie shouted. She seemed thrilled to put an end to Sabrina's charades. "Kurt, why don't you get the pies? Sabrina, can I talk to you in the kitchen?" She grabbed her best friend by the arm and pulled her into the next room.

"What do you think you're doing?" Roxie whispered to Sabrina once they were alone. "You promised to make yourself scarce."

"Oh I did, didn't I," Sabrina said, embarrassed. "I guess I forgot. We all seemed to be having so much fun."

"No, we weren't," Roxie assured her. "Come on. Kurt and I need to get to know each other better. Do you know he hasn't even tried to kiss me yet?"

"His lips don't move that way," Sabrina muttered under her breath.

"What?" Roxie asked her.

"I said, 'Maybe this is your lucky day,'" Sabrina said, covering for herself.

"Not if you don't leave," Roxie told her.

"But . . ."

Before Sabrina could finish her sentence, she was interrupted by a loud voice coming from the living room. "Look, Mac, you either pay me with real cash, or I take the pies back, okay?"

Sabrina and Roxie dashed into the living room.

"Tennis anyone?" Kurt asked.

The pizza deliveryman was in no mood for a tennis match. "I'll show you what you can do with a tennis racket," he told Kurt.

"Um, what seems to be the trouble, sir?" Sabrina asked, inching her way between Kurt and the increasingly angry deliveryman.

"This joker tried to pay for the pizza with toy money." The deliveryman waved a stack of lavender-colored bills at Sabrina. Every piece of paper had Kurt's or Betsy's photo where the picture of the president usually was.

"Oh Kurt, you're so funny," Sabrina said quickly. "Isn't he, Rox?"

Roxie didn't say anything. She was too busy staring from the purple money to the blank stare on Kurt's face.

Sabrina reached into her wallet and pulled out a twenty-dollar bill—the real, green kind. "Here ya go," she said. "Keep the change," she added, in an effort to keep the deliveryman from knocking Kurt's head from his neck. She figured seeing something like that would probably freak Roxie out.

As soon as Kurt took the pizza, Sabrina tried to

close the door. But Roxie was too quick for her. "Sorry you had to not eat and run," she said as she pushed Sabrina out into the cold autumn night.

Sabrina was depressed. Another twenty dollars gone. And she hadn't even gotten a single slice of pizza.

When Sabrina was bummed out, she went in search of ice cream. There was one freezer in town that always seemed to be stocked, and it was conveniently located right next door—at Hilda and Zelda's place.

"Anybody home?" Sabrina asked as she walked into her aunts' house. "Aunt Zelda? Aunt Hilda?"

No one greeted Sabrina as she came inside. In fact, the only sound she heard was one of hysterical sobbing.

The crying seemed to be coming from the kitchen. That was a natural, considering whoever it was sounded just as depressed as Sabrina.

"Save me some strawberry!" Sabrina shouted as she dashed through the dining room and into the kitchen.

Sure enough, there were three huge containers of ice cream sitting out on the counter. And in the middle of them all sat Salem. His little face was covered with ice cream, small bits of cookie dough, pistachio nuts, and chocolate chips.

"Aaargh," he cried as he stuck his little face into a pint of pistachio.

Sabrina sighed. "Can't you at least use a spoon?" she scolded him as she went into the freezer to pull out a pint of ice cream.

Salem held up a paw. "Do you see any thumbs here?" he demanded.

"Sheesh, sorry. Somebody got up on the wrong side of the litter box today," Sabrina snapped back.

"I don't sleep in my litter box," he told her. "And I have every right to be upset. I'm completely broke."

"Join the club," Sabrina said, chomping down on a frozen cherry. She stopped for a second. "Wait a minute. I thought you told me you were making a fortune on those Cattitude tapes."

"I was," Salem. "*Was* being the operative word. Didn't you see this evening's paper?"

Sabrina shook her head. "I was too busy entertaining Kurt and Roxie."

"Well, now's your chance to get caught up on current events," Salem told her. He used his paw to push the newspaper across the counter. Then he dug his face deep into the cookie dough ice-cream carton.

Sabrina looked at the paper. There was a photo of Harvey and some other Cattitude followers sitting in a tree. The headline read: CATTITUDE GOES CAPUT.

"'Local firefighters have been inundated with emergency calls from stranded teens recently, due to some advice offered on the enormously popular Cattitude tapes,'" Sabrina read aloud.

"'According to Police Chief Stephen Jeffries, "Our firefighters have been so busy rescuing stranded teenagers that we were two engines short at a fire on Surrey Road this morning. Luckily we were able to put out the blaze without anyone being injured. Nevertheless, this Cattitude craze is putting the public at great risk.

"'The fire department announced plans to sue the marketers of the Cattitude program if they do not cease distribution of their tapes immediately,'" Sabrina read aloud.

Salem put his paws over his ears. "Stop. I can't listen to this anymore! It's too painful. "

Sabrina obediently put down the paper and stopped reading. She looked at Salem. "I'm sorry," she said sympathetically. "I guess this is the end of your corporate empire."

"Tell me about it," Salem agreed.

"Well, at least you've made money on the tapes you've already sold," Sabrina suggested, trying to console the cat.

But Salem was beyond consolation. "That's all gone," he admitted.

"Gone?" Sabrina asked. "But you earned thousands of dollars."

"Money just burns a hole in my pocket, Sabrina. I ordered all sorts of things from the Abercrombie and Witch catalog. Do you know how expensive that store can be?"

"But that can't be all your money," Sabrina said.

"I already reinvested the rest into making more Cattitude tapes. It seemed liked a sure thing at the time. But now . . . well . . . I would have done better investing in swampland."

Sabrina sighed. "I could have told you this would happen, Salem. Every time you try one of these get-rich-quick schemes . . ."

"I wouldn't be so quick to throw out the I-told-you-so's, Sabrina," Salem commented. "I notice I'm not the only one digging into the frozen desserts around here."

Sabrina stuffed another spoonful of ice cream

into her mouth. "Do we have any whipped cream in the fridge?" she asked.

"Oooh, you must be really down," Salem said.

"It's this Roxie and Kurt thing. You think you're broke? I've gone through most of my bank account already, paying for Kurt's clothes and house and car and—"

"I could have told you this would happen. Every time you butt into people's lives . . . ," Salem began. He smiled wickedly.

"Stop with the I-told-you-so's." Sabrina made a face. "I get the point." She stopped to wipe a dribble of ice cream from her chin. "The point is, you can cease production of your tapes and that'll be the end of your problems. But as long as Roxie likes Kurt, I've got to keep spending."

"I don't see what she sees in that guy. He's a total airhead . . . literally," Salem remarked.

"I don't get it either. I think she just likes the fact that he likes her, and that he's only got eyes for her."

"Oh, that gets old fast," Salem assured her.

"Not fast enough," Sabrina argued, thinking of her empty wallet.

"Roxie's pretty smart," Salem assured Sabrina. "Sooner or later she's got to see Kurt for what he is."

"A doll?" Sabrina asked. "I hope not. That would be tough to explain."

"Well, not a doll, exactly," Salem said. "But as someone not worthy of her. Then once her crush is over—"

"Kurt's back to his original eleven-and-a-half-inch size," Sabrina finished his thought. Her face brightened. "You're right, Salem. I'm sure Roxie will come to her senses soon."

Salem nodded. "Of course she will. And in the meantime, could you pass the Rocky Road? I'm all out of pistachio."

Chapter 13

Sabrina waddled into the living room of her college house and plopped down on the couch. "That last pint of mint chip was definitely over the top," she moaned to herself as she picked up the TV remote.

But as soon as Sabrina had settled comfortably onto the sofa, there was a knock at the door. "Come in," she shouted, throwing the remote down on the coffee table. There was no way she was getting up again just to answer the door. Her stomach couldn't take any more sudden movements.

"Hey Sabrina," Harvey greeted her as he sauntered into the house.

His whiskerlike mustache was gone, and he was wearing a T-shirt and jeans.

Sabrina smiled. He looked like the old Harvey again. "Sorry about Cattitude," she told him.

"Oh, it's okay," Harvey assured her. "It had to end sometime."

"You don't mind giving up the popularity, fame, and glory of being the Cattitude Dude?"

Harvey shook his head. "You know, popularity's not what it looks like. It's a lot of work. You always have to be upbeat and friendly. It's like you can never be in a bad mood."

"So Cattitude wasn't all it was cracked up to be?" Sabrina asked.

"Actually, it really was a good program . . . other than that tree-climbing thing, anyway," Harvey assured her. "I'm more confident, and I realized that I don't need Morgan to be popular. I don't even really want to be popular. I'd rather have a few good friends who like me for me—not because I dated Morgan. And I'm eating better. Do you know how healthy fish is for you?"

Sabrina moved back a little on the couch. Fish might be good for you, but it had done nothing for Harvey's breath. "I'm glad for you, Harvey," she assured him. She reached into her pocket. "After-dinner mint?" she asked, pulling out a candy.

"Thanks," Harvey replied, taking it from her hand. "And did you notice my new jeans? No holes, no stains. I'm sticking to the whole good-grooming thing."

"Very nice," Sabrina assured him.

Harvey smiled at her. "So what do you say we go out and celebrate the new me? We can go for an ice-cream sundae. My treat."

Sabrina could feel her stomach turn over. "Ice cream?" she said weakly. "Not tonight, Harvey."

"Okay, how about . . . ?"

Before Harvey could offer another suggestion, Roxie came moping slowly into the house.

Sabrina sat up. "How was your date?" she asked nervously.

"Fine," Roxie replied in a decidedly noncommittal tone.

"Just 'fine'?" Sabrina asked.

Roxie walked over to the freezer. "Hey, who ate all my fudge swirl?" she demanded.

Sabrina moaned and clutched her stomach. "Can we stop all the ice-cream talk, please?" she asked.

Roxie grabbed a doughnut and plopped down in a chair. "What's eating you?" she asked.

"It's more like what I ate," Sabrina corrected her. "But never mind me. What's up with you and the comfort food? Didn't you get enough pizza at Kurt's house?"

"Oh plenty," Roxie assured her. "We shared the whole pie. And that's all we did."

"Oh." Sabrina nodded knowingly. "So, there was no good night kiss?" Harvey grimaced. "Okay," he said. "This is where I make an exit. See ya tomorrow, Sabrina."

Sabrina waited for Harvey to leave before she pumped Roxie for more info. "What happened?" she asked finally.

"Nothing happened . . . and I mean nothing. I tried to start a conversation with the guy, but he kept asking me if I wanted to play tennis or go to the beach."

"He's an athletic type," Sabrina told her.

"Whatever. Anyway, seeing his house just sort of put things into perspective for me."

"What do you mean?" Sabrina asked. She struggled to keep the excitement from her voice. Could it be that Salem had been right for once? Was the bloom really off the rose when it came to Roxie's romance?

"He just has so much stuff," Roxie explained. "I never realized how into possessions Kurt was. I mean, does a person really need a minivan *and* a convertible? And does everything have to be purple? There are other colors out there, you know."

Sabrina frowned. That minivan had cost her about fifty bucks. What a waste. "Now she tells me," she whispered under her breath.

"What?" Roxie asked.

"I said, 'You're telling me,'" Sabrina replied. "But at least he's really into you."

"Yeah, but just how many times can you hear that your hair looks nice?" Roxie countered. "Speaking of hair, did you notice how his never seems to move? I think he's just too perfect for me. He's kind of shallow. No offense. I know Kurt's your friend and all, but he just seems so plastic."

"Oh, no offense taken," Sabrina assured her. "I'm glad you guys had a good time while it lasted. So, did you break it off with him tonight?"

Roxie frowned. "I couldn't. He was being so nice . . . weird, but nice. And I just couldn't."

Sabrina looked curiously at Roxie. This was a side of her she'd never seen before.

"Would you like me to help?" Sabrina asked, a bit too eagerly.

Roxie smiled for the first time since she'd gotten

home. "Could you? I usually don't mind breaking up with guys—in fact, it's kind of fun to break up with some of the jerks I usually date. But Kurt's different. I don't want to hurt him."

Sabrina already had her coat on and was heading for the door. "Don't worry," she assured her best friend. "He won't feel a thing."

Chapter 14

Sabrina was so anxious to zap Kurt back to his original doll-size self that she didn't even take the time to run to her aunts' house. Instead, she let her magic do the walking. Zap! Within seconds she was standing outside the purple town house in her aunts' backyard.

Unfortunately, so was her aunt Zelda. "Sabrina, just the person I was hoping to see," the elder witch greeted her niece. "I was standing here admiring the architecture on our neighbors' home. Early twenty-first century, would you say?"

"Um . . . yeah."

Zelda nodded. "And such a unique building material. What would you call it?"

"Plastic," Sabrina replied. "I can explain, Aunt Zelda."

"I'm sure you can," Zelda said. "But you don't need to. I suspect this is a very large dollhouse for that very large doll you've been hanging around with."

"You're so smart, Aunt Zelda," Sabrina answered. Granted, she was shamelessly buttering up her aunt, but hey, it usually worked.

Just not this time.

"Well, it's got to go," Zelda ordered her. "We can't have a purple plastic house in the backyard. We're not zoned for it."

"I'm working on it, Aunt Zelda. Kurt will be gone in a minute, and then I can zap the house back to the way it was."

"How are you going to get rid of Kurt?" Zelda asked. "I thought you had to get rid of the crush."

"That's why I'm here," Sabrina assured her aunt. "Roxie's totally over Kurt. She asked me to end the whole mess for her."

"That's awfully convenient."

"I know," Sabrina replied enthusiastically. "I love it when things work out."

"Mmm-hmm," Zelda said.

Sabrina looked at her aunt curiously. She seemed strangely noncommittal about this whole zap-Kurt-back-to-size thing. Sabrina thought Zelda would have been happy that Sabrina's worries were over.

But Sabrina couldn't take the time to ponder Zelda's strange reaction to the news right now. She had to get rid of that walking, talking money pit. Quickly, Sabrina opened the door to Kurt's house. She found him sitting on the couch, listening to his favorite CD—the one that contained all the Kurt and Betsy jingles.

> *"Riding through the snow,*
> *in Kurt's romantic car.*
> *Betsy's by his side,*
> *as they drive so far.*
> *Their skis are ready to go, and*
> *they'll frolic in the snow.*
> *All this can be yours,*
> *for just a little dough."*

Sabrina winced at the lyrics. She wondered just how many parents had gone broke buying all of Kurt's and Betsy's accessories.

"Okay, Kurt, playtime's over," she told him as she flicked off the CD player.

"I love your hair," Kurt told her.

"Yeah, yeah, whatever," Sabrina said. She pointed

her finger in his direction. *"Roxie's grown tired of this, big guy, so now it's time to give shrinking a try,"* she chanted. *"Good-bye, Kurt, it's been a ball. Go back to being eleven and a half inches tall."*

There. That was pretty good. Sabrina wiggled her finger triumphantly and stood back. She waited for Kurt to shrink.

And waited.

And waited.

But Kurt didn't shrink.

"Betsy is the coolest!" he said. "I'll pick you up in my car."

"AUNT ZELDA!" Sabrina cried out.

"Sabrina, don't scream," Zelda told her. "I'm right here."

Sabrina turned to find her aunt standing in the doorway. "He won't shrink," she said.

"I can see that," Zelda replied.

"But Roxie's done with him. No more crush. So he should shrink, right?"

"Wrong," Zelda explained. "Roxie is over Kurt. But Kurt isn't over Roxie. He's still true blue where she's concerned. And until he wants to break it off as badly as she does, he'll stay exactly as he is."

Sabrina gulped. It wasn't like, "Let's just be

139

friends," was part of Kurt's vocabulary.

"But Salem said that once Roxie got tired of Kurt, I'd be able to turn him back," Sabrina whined.

"Who are you going to listen to—a witch with a Mensa IQ, or a cat?" Zelda asked her.

"You," Sabrina said.

"Good. Now you're going to have to work on getting Kurt to move on with his life . . . such as it is. In the meantime, get rid of this giant dollhouse. It's the ugliest color I've ever seen."

"Purple is my favorite color," Kurt commented.

"Get rid of him, too!" Zelda shouted as she slammed the purple door behind her.

Roxie's eyes grew small and angry the moment Sabrina walked into their house—probably because Kurt was right behind her. "Uh, Sabrina," Roxie said through gritted teeth, "I thought you were going to help me with my little problem." She forced herself to smile in Kurt's direction. "Hi there, Kurt."

"Tennis anyone?" Kurt replied.

Roxie rolled her eyes.

"Rox, can I talk to you in the kitchen?" Sabrina asked. "Kurt, you stay here, okay?"

"I'll pick you up in my car," he replied.

"We have a little problem," Sabrina whispered to Roxie once the girls were alone. "He's still crazy about you. He doesn't want to let you go."

"Did you tell him it just wasn't working?"

Sabrina nodded. "I tried the whole way over here."

"Well, what did he say?"

Sabrina shrugged. "What could he say? He said, 'Let's go to the beach.'"

Roxie frowned. "Sounds like Kurt."

"You're going to have to make him stop liking you," Sabrina told Roxie. "Any way you can."

"How am I supposed to do that?"

"How do you break up with anyone?" Sabrina asked her. "You've done this before."

"Oh, but that's too mean," Roxie insisted. "He's actually a nice guy. Stupid, but nice."

"Be as mean as you want," Sabrina assured her.

Roxie looked surprised. "I thought Kurt was your friend. Why do you want me to hurt him?"

"I don't want you to hurt him. I just want you to get rid of him. It's meaner to keep him hanging on, don't you think?" Sabrina took a deep breath. That was quick thinking.

"I guess you're right," Roxie replied slowly.

"You know I am," Sabrina assured her. "Now go

out there and give the guy the full Roxie treatment."

"Okay," Roxie said doubtfully. "I only hope it will work. The guy is awfully nuts about me."

"'Nuts' is the word for it," Sabrina agreed as she opened the fridge and pulled out a soda. Then she walked into the bedroom she shared with Roxie and shut the door. She didn't want to be around when the big bomb hit.

"Kurt, look, this just isn't going to work," Roxie explained as she sat down in a chair across the room and looked him straight in his expressionless eyes. "We're too different. You've got to move on."

"Let's go to the beach," Kurt replied.

Roxie sighed. "Okay, no more Mr. Nice Guy," she murmured to herself. She got up and walked toward the kitchen.

"Want to share a soda?" Kurt asked her.

"No. I do not want to share a soda. I don't want to go for pizza. I don't want to dance. Get it?" she barked back.

"Tennis anyone?" Kurt suggested.

That was the last straw. Roxie no longer felt any sympathy for Kurt. All she felt was frustration, and a slight bit of rage. "How could I ever have liked you?"

she asked. "You're completely empty-headed."

"Purple is my favorite color."

"Is there anything in there?" Roxie reached over and gave him a slight tap on the top of the head. A hollow sound rang back at her. "Okay," she said slowly. "That was weird."

"Let's party."

"No," Roxie insisted. "No parties. No purple cars. And I definitely don't want to hear about that Betsy chick. I just want you to leave."

"I love your hair."

"AAARGH!" Roxie shouted as she ran toward her bedroom and slammed the door behind her.

Sabrina looked up as Roxie stormed into the room. "All done?" she asked with hope.

"Not exactly," Roxie said. "He's still here. And he still loves my hair."

"Oh no!" Sabrina exclaimed. "What am I going to do now?"

"Excuse me?" Roxie asked. "And how exactly is this about you?"

Sabrina blushed. "I mean, what are we going to do now? I just feel responsible because I'm the one who introduced you to Kurt."

Roxie sat down beside Sabrina. "Don't feel bad,"

she said. "I mean, you were just trying to help. And I have to admit it was nice having a guy be so totally into me. But I think it has to be the right guy, otherwise, it just won't work. And Kurt is definitely not the right guy." She paused for a minute. "Do you know why his ex-girlfriend broke up with him? Was he this smothering with her, too?"

"Betsy didn't exactly break up with him . . . ," Sabrina began. She stopped midsentence. "Oh my goodness! That's it!" she exclaimed as she leaped off her bed and raced to put on her shoes.

"Where are you going?" Roxie demanded.

"To the mall!" Sabrina shouted excitedly.

"Now?" Roxie demanded. "In the middle of my crisis?"

Chapter 15

☆

"Hurry up, Kurt," Sabrina demanded as she practically dragged the six-foot-tall muscleman through the mall. "They're going to close any minute."

"Do you want to dance?" Kurt asked her.

Sabrina didn't answer. She simply turned the corner and raced toward the toy store. As she reached the front, a salesperson was already bringing down the gate that covered the front window. "Sorry, we're closing," she told Sabrina.

"But we have two more minutes," Sabrina insisted. She shoved her watch in front of the salesperson's face. "Please. I just need one thing. That's all."

The saleswoman barely heard her. She was too busy staring at Kurt's plastic-perfect features. "Okay," she murmured. "You can go in. But he has to stay out here with me."

"I love your hair," Kurt said.

Sabrina left the saleswoman blushing as she raced past the door and down the purple Betsy aisle. Quickly, she grabbed a small rectangular package from the shelf and hurried to the counter.

"You again?" the cashier asked as he took Sabrina's money and placed her toy in a bag. "Don't you think you're a little old to be playing with dolls?"

Sabrina nodded. "You have no idea," she assured him as she grabbed the bag and ran from the store.

"You know, I've always loved purple myself," the saleswoman was saying flirtatiously as Sabrina approached Kurt. "It's such a regal color, don't you think?"

"Let's go for pizza," Kurt replied.

"Not now," Sabrina told Kurt as she grabbed him by the arm. "We're going back to my aunts' house. I have a big surprise for you!"

"Sabrina!" Hilda remarked as her niece raced up the stairs without even so much as a hello. "Nice to see you too."

"Hi, Aunt Hilda," Sabrina shouted down the stairs.

Hilda switched off the TV and followed Sabrina

upstairs. She took one look at Kurt and swooned. "Well hello, mister," she said. "My name's Hilda. I'm Sabrina's aunt, but everyone says we look just like sisters."

"Do you want to dance?" Kurt asked.

"I'd love to," Hilda agreed. She started dancing—right in the hallway.

"Aunt Hilda, stop," Sabrina warned her.

"Why?" Hilda asked. "This is the latest dance."

The noise in the hallway brought Zelda from her room. "Could you please stop stomping around out here?" she demanded, standing between Hilda and Kurt. "I'm trying to go over the notes from my conference this afternoon."

"Excuse me. What are you doing?" Hilda asked. "This young stud muffin and I were having a moment. You've interrupted us. And, by the way, I wasn't stomping, I was dancing!"

Zelda looked over at Kurt. "Is he still here? Sabrina, I thought you were going to take care of this problem."

"I was," Sabrina said. She waved the toy store bag in Zelda's face. "I have the solution right here."

"So what's stopping you?" Zelda asked.

Sabrina pointed to Hilda. "She is."

Zelda shook her head. "Hilda, don't you know a doll when you see one?"

"Obviously. I was dancing with him, wasn't I?"

"No, I mean a real doll," Zelda said. "Kurt here is a plastic doll that Sabrina brought to life for Roxie. Not only is he too young for you—he's plastic. Anyone could see that."

Sabrina choked back a laugh. Zelda had been pretty taken in by Kurt when she'd first met him. But Sabrina wasn't about to bring that up right now. Aunt Zelda was angry enough about Kurt and the purple house.

"Come on, Kurt," Sabrina said as she dragged him into her room, leaving her aunts to argue in the hall. "Let's get this over with."

Sabrina reached into the bag and pulled out her purchase—an eleven and a half inch talking Betsy doll. She carefully took the doll out of the box.

The sudden movement in the room woke Salem, who had been sleeping on the windowsill. He opened one eye and looked disapprovingly at Sabrina. "Not another doll," he moaned. "What, are you bringing this one to life for Harvey?"

Sabrina didn't answer the cat. Instead, she smiled at Kurt. "This is for you."

Kurt took the small fashion doll in his hands. "Betsy is the coolest," he said softly. He stroked her long, straight hair. "I love your hair."

"You missed her, didn't you?" Sabrina asked Kurt.

"Purple is my favorite color," he replied. "Betsy is the coolest."

"Yes, she is," Sabrina agreed. "And I can give her back to you."

"Sabrina, I don't think zapping Betsy to life is going to solve your problem," Salem warned.

"Don't worry, Salem," Sabrina assured him. "I have it all under control."

"Do you want to be with Betsy forever, Kurt?" she asked the doll.

"Betsy is the coolest," he assured Sabrina.

"Okay, then. Let's get to it," Sabrina agreed. She pointed her finger at Kurt.

> *"Betsy is Kurt's one and only.*
> *Roxie won't mind being lonely.*
> *So forget about being six feet tall.*
> *Let's make Kurt nice and small."*

Zap! There was a flash of light. And then, suddenly, Kurt was gone. Well, not gone actually, just smaller.

He and Betsy were exactly the same size—eleven and a half inches tall.

"What's going on in here?" Zelda asked as she peeked into Sabrina's room. Instantly she spotted the two small dolls on the bed. "Oh, good! You did it!"

Sabrina smiled proudly. "Once again, true love has conquered all."

"What are you talking about?" Hilda asked. "Where's Kurt?"

"With Betsy," Sabrina assured her. "Right where he should be."

"Oh, I see," Zelda said. "That's pretty clever."

"I don't see. *What's* clever?" Hilda asked.

"Betsy was Kurt's first love," Sabrina explained. "And when he saw her again, he could never belong to anyone else. Once he held Betsy in his arms, he forgot all about Roxie. After that, it was easy to zap him back."

"We've got quite an intelligent niece," Zelda told Hilda.

"She gets that from my side of the family," Hilda replied.

"We're on the same side of the family, Hilda."

"Don't remind me," Hilda said. She looked around the room. "I'm glad this all worked out for you, Sabrina. I only have one question. What are you going to do with all these purple clothes and that dollhouse?"

Sabrina looked around the room. There were Kurt clothes everywhere. The now-small purple town house sat in the corner of the room, with all its furniture intact. And, of course, there were Talking Kurt and Betsy, who sat side by side on the edge of the bed.

"I think I'll take this stuff over to that family shelter on Main Street. I'll bet some of the little girls over there would love to play with Betsy and Kurt, just the way I did."

Salem leaped down from the windowsill. As he landed, his paw touched a small button on Kurt's back.

"Betsy is the coolest," the doll said.

Chapter 16

"**S**ee you later," Morgan called to Sabrina and Roxie as she grabbed her long, sky blue cardigan and raced for the door. "Don't wait up."

"You're in a good mood," Sabrina said.

"Why not? Now that everyone's gotten over this Cattitude thing, life's back to normal. I'm at the top of the food chain, and Harvey . . . well, he's back with the two of you."

"And where would that be?" Roxie demanded.

Morgan shrugged and pretended to zip her lips shut. "If you can't say anything nice . . ." She let her voice drift off as she let the door slam behind her.

Sabrina noticed the look of seething anger on Roxie's face. "Relax, someday Morgan will get hers."

"She's already getting hers . . . and mine . . . and

yours. Once again, it's a Saturday night and we don't have dates," Roxie reminded her.

"I could always try to track down Kurt for you," Sabrina said.

"That's okay," Roxie said. "I think it's great that he's joined the Peace Corps. And that little village with no phones is perfect for him. He's not exactly a brilliant conversationalist."

Sabrina smiled. She was relieved that Roxie had bought the story she'd concocted about Kurt's sudden disappearance. Now if she could only come up with an excuse for the missing purple house before the next time Roxie dropped by Hilda and Zelda's place.

Roxie stood up and slipped on her leather jacket. "You're sure you don't want to come to the meeting with me?"

Sabrina shook her head. "I'm not really into that whole save-the-squid movement," she told Roxie. "But you go ahead. I'll be fine here."

"You sure?" Roxie said.

Sabrina nodded.

"Okay. I guess I should get going. But I feel bad leaving you here all alone."

"Oh, I won't be alone," Sabrina assured her. "I'm going to hang out with an old friend."

"Oh, who?" Roxie began. Then she stopped herself. "Never mind. I've already gotten in enough trouble with one of your old friends."

Sabrina giggled.

"Have fun. See ya later," Roxie said as she headed for the door.

"Give my best to the squid-savers," Sabrina called after her.

As soon as the house was empty, Sabrina went into the bedroom she shared with Roxie. She waited a few minutes—just to make sure her roommates weren't returning. Then she bent down and peeked under her bed.

"Oooh. I really have to clean under here. Aaaachoo!" She sneezed as a giant dust bunny rolled out from beneath the bed frame. Sabrina quickly tossed aside a few unmatched socks, a pair of dirty jeans she'd forgotten to wash, and a half-eaten, dust-covered pack of Life Savers. She smiled brightly when she finally found what she was looking for.

A small, plastic, purple carrying case.

Sabrina grabbed the case and hopped back up on her bed. She opened the top and pulled out her old Snowbunny Betsy doll. She'd gladly given the children at the shelter everything she'd bought for Kurt, as well as the new Talking Betsy and Kurt dolls. But she couldn't bear to give away her old Betsy, or any of the doll's original "smashing fashions."

Sabrina pulled a teeny purple comb from one of the drawers in the carrying case, and began to twist Betsy's hair into a tight French braid.

"It's nice to spend an evening with an old friend," Sabrina said, sighing contentedly.

About the Author

☆

☆

Nancy Krulik is the best-selling author of more than one hundred books for children and young adults. She's been a Sabrina fan since she was a kid, and has especially fond memories of reading *Sabrina, the Teenage Witch* comic books late at night under the covers with a flashlight.

Like Sabrina, Nancy admits to having played with fashion dolls as a child. What she remembers most about her dolls is that the shoes always disappeared, and the dolls often seemed to lose their heads.

Today, Nancy lives in Manhattan with her husband, composer Daniel Burwasser, their two children, a tortoise, and a chocolate-and-white cocker spaniel. (Just don't tell Salem about the cocker spaniel—you know how he is about dogs!)